HATCHER

ERNEST ROBERSON SR.

ERNEST ROBERSON SR-

HATCHER

BY: ERNEST ROBERSON SR.

ERNEST ROBERSON SR-

ERNEST ROBERSON SR-

HATCHER

This book is a work of fiction. Names, characters, places, and incidents are products of the author's imagination and are not to be construed as real. Any resemblance to actual events, locales, organizations, or persons living or dead, is entirely coincidental.

Hacher

Cover By: Trient Press

Published by Trient Press: 3375 S Rainbow Blvd, #81710, SMB 13135, Las Vegas, NV 89180

978-1-953975-72-0   Hard Cover

ERNEST ROBERSON SR-

978-1-953975-73-7   Paperback

978-1-953975-64-5   Ebook - EPUB

Ordering Information:
Quantity sales. Special discounts are available on quantity purchases by corporations, associations, and others. For details, contact the publisher at the address above.
Orders by U.S. trade bookstores and wholesalers. Please contact Trient Press: Tel: (775) 996-3844; or visit www.trientpress.com.

Printed in the United States of America.

BOOK ONE

DEADLY LESSONS

ERNEST ROBERSON SR-

ERNEST ROBERSON SR-

CHAPTER ONE

It was 5:30 on a humid Friday evening in mid-July with a thunderhead forming in the south. Jon Wells had packed his belongings stood in the foyer of his parents' home, waiting for his friends to pick him up. Like his friends, Jon had just graduated from Wheeler County High, and they agreed to have one last adventure before going their separate ways. A vehicle rumbled down the driveway, and Jon picked up his two brown suitcases from the tiled floor, ready to rush out and join his friends. To his disappointment, his mother opened the door.

Jon's father stood at the kitchen table with one hand in the pocket of his suit trousers while the cradled a crystal tumbler. "You kids won't be drinking and driving, right son?" he asked, shaking the tumbler just enough to make the pair of ice cubes clink against the sides of the glass. As always, he'd mixed the whiskey with too much cherry juice, and the liquid in the glass took on a reddish hue in the soft lights of the chandelier overhead.

"No, sir," Jon answered. The irony was not lost on him. His father's law degree from the University of Georgia hung in the home-office, and he'd built up a reputation as a brutal defense attorney. His son, however, was a different story. Jon knew that if he ever got into any trouble with the law, his father wouldn't be there to save him. He'd always been hard on Jon, especially when it came to his grades, and Jon begrudgingly accepted this as his father's way of trying to make a good man out of him.

His mother breezed in and was about to close the door behind her when a horn blew from outside. "Is that your ride, dear?" she asked. "They must've been right behind me."

Jon looked out the front door to see his friends in a white Tahoe with the windows rolled down, waving for him to come on.

"Yep," Jon said. "See you all in a week!"

"You kids have fun at Camp Okefenokee," his mother said, hugging him as he attempted to step out onto the porch.

"It's not a camp, mom. It's a National Wildlife Refuge," Jon replied.

"Don't sass your mother," his father said.

"Sorry," Jon replied. "Just saying."

Jon's father sat at the kitchen table. "Did you pack that protection I asked you about last night?" He adjusted the knot of his tie, although there was no need. As if in response to this, Jon grabbed the shirttail of western-style work shirt, but did not tuck it in.

Hanging her keys on the peg by the front door, Jon's mother rolled her eyes, but Jon just laughed it off. "Yes, dad," he said, patting the back pocket of his jeans. "Wouldn't leave home without it."

"I don't understand why he doesn't tuck in that shirt," his mother said as she watched him make his way down the driveway. "It looks so nice when he tucks it in."

"Aw, let him do," his father said. "He's hanging out with his friends."

The door clicked as his mother shut it. "I'm surprised you didn't remind him, Mr. GQ."

"Hell, he's grown now," his father said, sipping from his tumbler. "If the worst he ever does is wear his shirt untucked, we've done a good job raising him."

Jon put his luggage in the back of the white Tahoe and got in behind the driver's seat. Jim Stewart sat behind the wheel, gripping the leather steering wheel cover. The Tahoe wasn't new, but Jim was proud of it regardless; he'd worked two summers as a bag-boy at the Piggly Wiggly to buy it, and it treated it like it was a Rolls Royce.

Amy Sparks sat in the passenger seat with her bare feet on the dash. She turned and grinned at Jon as they pulled out onto the highway. "So how are you doing, Jon?" she asked.

"Good," Jon replied, watching the green shimmering polish adorning Amy's toes. "Just ready to escape from society for a little while."

"Hell, we all are," Amy's sister Lisa said as Jim drove out of the half-circle concrete driveway.

Mike Smith sat behind Amy, staring out of the window.

"You're mighty quiet, Mike," Jon said. "Something wrong?".

. "No," Mike said.

"It'll take us about an hour to get there," Jim said.

As a light rain began to fall, Amy said, ""I'm glad that we already made reservations."

"So we should get there between 6:30 or 6:45 then?" Mike asked.

"Should," Jim replied as he looked in the rear-view mirror. "If we can beat this rain."   Jon leaned to his right just enough to read the speedometer as it hit 70 mph and held firm, making the droplets of rain roll off to the side of the windshield. Amy plugged her phone into the stereo and played the same road trip playlist they'd listened to since they could drive.

"Aww, this same old shit?" Mike groaned.

"Come on, Mike," Amy said. "It'll bring back memories." She opened a navigation app on her phone and entered the address.

"Yeah," Mike muttered, "memories from when we were sixteen. We're not kids anymore."

The five said nothing as the Tahoe's tires hummed on the highway.

*　*　*

"Almost there," Jim said.

"Watch the road signs for 177 South," Amy said, looking at her phone. "My GPS is acting up. I'm playing my music offline already."

"We're out in the middle of nowhere. That's why," Mike said.

Jim looked over his shoulder at Mike. "What's wrong with you, sunshine? You upset you won't be able to crush heads on the ballfield now that you've graduated?"

"Shit, I'll do even better at Middle Georgia."

"That's what I'm talking about," Jim said, looking back to the road. "Your records will stand for years. Well, at least till I have a kid and he busts them wide open. How about you, Jon? You gonna graduate from UGA with Honors, be a lawyer like your old man?"

"Yeah," Jon said. "Why not?" he watched out of Mike's window for the 177 South road sign.

"What about you, Jim?" Jon asked.

"Hell, I knew what I was gonna do since I was a little kid. Farm, same as my dad."

"What's going to be your main crop?" Lisa asked, rolling her eyes.

"Tobacco," Jim replied. "My nana was ninety-five when she died. Smoked three packs a day. All that shit about smoking causing cancer is made up."

"All that shit you talk is made up, more like it," Lisa said.

Jim scowled, but laughed. "Hey now, not in front of the boys!" he said, grinning.

"Is it weird that I'm going to miss high school?" Amy said.

"You're a weirdo anyway, "Lisa said. "I won't miss the school in general, but Mrs. Brown and Mrs. Barker were okay."

"How about Mr. and Mrs. Collins?" Jim asked.

"Mrs. Collins was tough, but I'm going to miss Coach Collins," Mike replied. "You just liked Mrs. Collins 'cause you wanted some after school tutoring with her."

"I think all you boys did," Amy said.

"Mr. Black was a good principal," Jon said.

"Nice way to change the subject," Lisa said. "He was cool principal, I guess. Except for that time he busted me for smoking in my car."

"There's 177 South," Amy said, tapping on the window with her index finger.

Jim glanced at the green numbers on the radio's clock. "6:05," he said.

"You all do know that there's alligators, panthers, snakes, and bears out in these woods?" Jon asked.

"No shit," Jim said. "So no wandering off by yourselves."

"You gonna protect me from all the critters, big man?" Mike asked.

"Hell, no. I'm gonna let them eat your sorry ass."

Amy turned the music down a few notches. "Hush, everybody," she said. "There's a dirt road up here we need to catch."

"It's coming up," Mike said. "Go ahead and slow down."

Amy turned around in her seat as Jim slowed the Tahoe. "You've been out this way?" she asked Mike.

"Not really, but I know some folks that have. Should be right up here."

"If I can see it through this goddamn rain," Jim said.

"There it is," Lisa said, pointing at a brown wooden sign reading "Okefenokee National Wildlife Refuge" in yellow letters.

"Shit," Jim said as he hit the brakes and eased onto the road. "Almost missed it."

As soon as the Tahoe's tires hit the dirt road, all five of its passengers heard the thick clay slap the undercarriage. "It should only be a few miles now," Amy said. A few specks of mud flew up and stuck to her window.

"Fuck this clay road," Jim said, gripping the steering wheel with both hands. "Feels like I'm driving through soup."

"Sure got dark in a hurry," Mike said, looking out of the window. The trees grew larger and thicker as Jim pushed down the road, managing only 35 mile per hour as the Tahoe slid left and right. He tried to laugh it off, but he laughed a little too hard and a little too long as he fought the wheel to keep the Tahoe straight in the road. Amy sensed this and turned off the radio completely so Jim could concentrate.

"Did anybody see that?" Mike asked.

"Hush, Mike," Amy scolded. "This is no time to play games."

The others tried to catch a glimpse of the road through the battering rain.

"I'm serious," Mike continued.

The Tahoe reared upward, and its passengers scrambled for something to grab onto as the it rolled onto one side for moment before righting itself in the ditch.

ERNEST ROBERSON SR-

ERNEST ROBERSON SR-

CHAPTER TWO

Jon looked out of his window as specks of red clay mud peppered the side of the Tahoe before the rain washed it clean.   "It's only spinning down, Jim," he said. "We might be able to push it out."

"I'm for real," Mike said. "Did nobody see what I saw?"

Lisa leaned forward between Jim and Amy. "There's gotta be a house close by," she said. "Check and see if anybody lives out here."

Amy tapped on her phone's screen but shook her head. "No service," she said.

"Mine's busted," said Jon. "Must've stomped on it when we wrecked."

"Should've kept that case I gave you for your birthday," said Lisa.

"Hey!" Mike yelled.

Everyone stopped and looked to Mike. "I know somebody lives out here," he said.

"You know somebody out here?" Jim asked.

"No, I mean I know somebody lives out here. I was trying to say something, but y'all wouldn't listen. I saw this guy running in the woods. Nobody else saw him?"

"Shit," Jim said, "I was too busy looking at the road."

"Me, too," said Jon. "What did this guy look like?"

Mike held his palm against the window glass and pulled it away, leaving an imprint of fog on the glass. "Rain's letting up," he said.

"Mike," Jon said, "are you just fucking with us, or did you really see something?"

"I couldn't get a good look at him through the rain, but he was wearing all blue," Mike answered. "Looked liked his clothes were all ripped up. And he was wearing gloves. Real big dude."

Lisa leaned back against Jon. "Yep," she said, "he's bullshitting."

"It's what I saw."

Leaning over the steering wheel, Jim howled with laughter. "You expect me to believe that?" he said as he caught his breath.

Mike sat up straight, trying to lock eyes with Jim in the rearview mirror. "I don't see what's so funny."

"You had a problem with my music because you said we're not kids anymore," Amy said, not bothering to turn around and face Mike as she spoke, "but now you're trying to pull that ghost story shit on us?"

"What ghost story?" Mike said.

"Come on," Jon said. "Even my parents know the one about Hatchetface."

"Well," Mike sneered, "not all of us had mommies and daddies to pass on ghost stories. Besides, I was too busy playing ball to tell ghost stories, anyway."

"I don't want to talk about it," Lisa said, shaking her head. "It gives me the creeps."

Mike opened his door. "No way in hell we're pulling this out," he said.

All of them opened their doors, and Jim slapped the windshield when he saw both passenger-side tires half-covered in clay. "Well, there's still a little daylight left," he said. "I say we get going while the rain's letting up." The five unloaded from the Tahoe, closed the doors, and Jim locked it. Dusk neared with an overcast of clouds.

*　　　*　　　*

As darkness fell, Lisa whined, "God, I wish somebody'd come by and pick us up."

"At least the rain's stopped," Amy said. "Let's keep going. Somebody's gotta live around here. Anybody got service on your phones yet?"

"You just asked us that ten minutes ago," Jim said. "My battery's dead, anyhow."

"Shit," Mike said. "I left my charger in the truck."

"Me, too," Lisa said.

"Look guys," Amy said, pointing, "there's a light in the woods!"

A strip of what appeared to be white sand shone pale even in the dark, and through the wall of trees a light shimmered.

"Looks like a road," Jim said. "Hard to tell."

"Gotta be," said Jon. "If there's light, there's people."

Mike laughed. "Great," he said, "we get to spend the night with a bunch of swamp-dwelling rednecks."

Lisa slapped him on the arm. "Look on the bright side," she said, "there might be a cute girl you can talk the panties off of."

"Sure, if her brother hasn't called dibs on her already."

"Follow me," said Jim.

The rain fell harder as the five cautiously walked along the sandy road, feeling their feet shift beneath them slightly, headed for the light.

*   *   *

They came to the yard of a two-story house, then climbed the steps onto the porch and Jon knocked on the front door. An ancient-looking woman open the door, holding a kerosene lantern. The lantern cast its feeble light onto the porch, and Lisa read a sign beside the door that read "Joshua 24:15," and underneath this another sign reading "The Lewis'."

"May I help you?" the woman asked in a soft, low voice.

"Yes, you might can," Jon said.

"Well, don't just stand out there," the woman said, "come on."

Lisa closed the door behind everyone. The elderly woman sat in a rocking chair that faced the front door. The five seated themselves on a brown cloth couch and matching loveseat which faced the elderly woman. Jim began telling her what had happened, and where they were headed. Lisa noticed the flooring of the house was bare wood, and the slight spaces between some of the floorboards showed her the ground below. She had also noticed that there weren't any light fixtures or light switches in the house.

"You all don't have power out here?" Lisa interrupted.

"No, dear we don't."

"What was your name again?" Amy asked.

"Helen. Helen Lewis."

"Well, Mrs. Helen could you give us a ride to the camp?" Lisa asked.

"I have no way of going myself, but you all are welcome to stay the night," Helen replied.

"We don't want impose, ma'am," Jim said, "but we really don't have a choice."

"No imposition," said Helen.

She grabbed up the lantern from the end table and led the five upstairs. "You boys can stay in this room," she said. She pulled a box of matches from the left pocket of her robe lit the oil lamps in a large room, then left out of that room. She went back into the hallway where Amy and Lisa stood waiting and led them a few feet down the hallway next door to another room. "And you girls can spend the night in here," she said, and lit an oil lamp in this room. "Good night," she said, then left.

Amy shut the wooden door, but left the deadbolt unlocked. She looked at Lisa sitting on the bed.

"Something's wrong here," Lisa said. "Can't you see?"

"You're just creeped out still from what Mike said. He's screwing with you."

Amy sat beside her on the bed, but Lisa stood and locked the deadbolt. "No, Amy," she said, "I don't like this.

Any of it. Who still lives without electricity? How do they cook? What do they cook? They have no well, which means they have no running water."

"Let's just sleep on it tonight, and we'll be gone tomorrow," Amy said, lying on the bed.

Lisa sat in a wooden chair by the bed, listening through the thin walls as the three boys discussed how to get the Tahoe out of the ditch.

* * *

Amy rolled over and grabbed her phone from the floor. She picked it up and read "5:47 on the screen." "Shit," she said, "left it on all night." She got out of the bed and looked out of the curtain-less, blind-less window. A pale light struggled to push its way over the horizon, but she knew it would be at least another hour before the sun was up.

Lisa slept in the chair beside the bed, and Amy nudged her.

"Let's go downstairs and talk with Helen," she said.

Lisa rubbed her eyes and tried to focus. "What the hell are you talking about?" she asked. "What time is it?"

"Almost six in the morning."

"She's probably still asleep."

"One way to find out."

Amy knocked lightly on the wooden door of the boys' bedroom. The girls waited, and then she knocked again. After a few minutes she was about to knock again as Jim opened the bedroom door.

"What's wrong?" he asked.

"Nothing's wrong," Lisa replied.

"We wanted to go downstairs and talk with Helen. We feel out of place here, Jim," Amy said.

As she said what needed to be said, Mike and Jon came to door as well.

"Give us a few minutes to dress, and we'll all go downstairs," Jim said closing the door.

Downstairs they saw Helen in her rocking chair, and they all sat on the brown couch and loveseat just as before. All, that is, except for Lisa, who stood in front of the darkened brick fireplace to the left of Helen's chair.

"Mrs. Helen," Lisa called out.

"Yes, dear?"

"Sorry to wake you."

"I wasn't asleep, darling." Helen rocked gently in her rocking chair. "What can I do for you?"

"We forgot to ask you if this is the only house on this road," Jim said.

"No, son, but the other homes around here is abandoned."

"I saw somebody running in the woods," Mike interjected. "Do you know who that might have been?"

Lisa shot him a stern look.

Helen stopped rocking. "What did he look like?"

"He was a real tall, big guy," Mike answered, "wearing all blue, ripped up clothes. Looked like he was wearing gloves."

"I don't know no one has been in these woods since last year," Helen responded. "That's when about six campers were going to Camp Okefenokee like yourselves."

"What happened to them?" Mike asked.

"It's not a pretty story, dear."

"What happened, Helen?" Jon asked.

"They was teenagers, early twenties maybe. They picked up a boy who was along about nineteen on the dirt road. Anyhow, they got to the camp and settled in. They smoked their mary jane and drank their beers. You know, the stuff kids do. So the stranger which they picked up, they gave a bag to him then blindfolded him, and led him into the woods."

"Snipe hunting?" Jim asked.

"Yes, snipe hunting," Helen replied. "I take it you've heard the story, son?"

"I've heard different versions of it, yes ma'am. But go on."

"The boy was mangled by the alligators, panthers, snakes, and bears."

"Did he die?" Lisa asked.

"I'd imagine so. But some say he's still out there, and that this part of the reservation is now cursed."

Headlights beaming brightly in the yard got everyone's attention as they looked out the front windows.

*　　　*　　　*

A tall, muscular man walked into the house. He looked at Helen, then the others one by one afterward sitting on the brown couch and loveseat. Mike, who'd become adept at measuring up another man from his time playing football, estimated that this man was around 6' 2'', and at least 220 lbs. Though he was obviously an older man, he'd reached a point of age at which it was impossible to accurately judge his years.

"Everyone," Helen said, "this is my husband, John."

"That y'all's Tahoe in the ditch down the road?" John said.

"Yes, sir," Jim replied.

"Well come on then," John demanded. "I got a wrecker out back."

John retrieved the Tahoe with his wrecker and the five stood in the front yard of the Lewis house, watching as the wrecker lowered the Tahoe to the grass. The boys helped John unhook everything as the first rays of sunlight spilled over the trees.

"Do we owe you all anything?" they all asked John.

"No," John insisted. "You all best get going before it gets dark again."

They loaded up in the Tahoe, and Jim pulled back on to the dirt road, still spongy but passable. Jim said the only thing said since they had left the Lewis house: "I think it's all a myth."

"What? Lisa asked. "The curse and all?"

"Absolutely. I bet she tells everybody that. Hell, that's probably where the whole story started, some old crazy hag with nothing better to do than try and scare campers."

As the five finally pulled up to the campground, they saw four cabins in the headlights which numbered one through four. Jim left on the headlights as everyone unloaded their luggage from the back of the Tahoe. Lisa and Amy took cabin one. Inside, Amy found and lit the kerosene lantern which gave off enough light for the small cabin. Jim took cabin two, Jon cabin three, and Mike cabin four. When all of the lanterns were lit, Jim turned off the Tahoe's lights, locked it, and walked towards his cabin. Almost there, he stopped, startled by the sound of a twig snapping somewhere in the distance He looked around with his flashlight but saw nothing. He shrugged, then headed towards his cabin.

Exhausted, they settled in. The rain set in again, and lightning flashed, somewhat obscured by the oak trees stretching over the cabins. One by one, each of the five set their lanterns on the floor of their respective cabins, casting five shimmering lights, and fell asleep.

ERNEST ROBERSON SR-

CHAPTER THREE

The sun rose behind the cabins and the sky was clear as the campers woke up several minutes apart.

Jim was the first to venture outside. He looked around at the steps of his cabin and saw a fire pit encircled by rocks. Four two-person wooden benches encircled the fire pit. To the south was the lake, complete with a wooden dock. In the growing light, Jim also noticed a wooden outhouse situated not far from a clear trail that was also lined with rocks. Mike and Jon had come outside, and they joined him in the middle of the campsite as he stood at the fire pit.

"The girls up?" Mike asked.

"I suppose they are," Jim replied. "I haven't heard from them yet."

"What do we need to do?" Jon asked.

"Let's get some firewood now so it'll be dry in case it rains again," Jim said. "Then we'll unload the coolers and pots from the Tahoe."

They hauled the coolers and pots to the fire pit. As they were heading into the woods to gather firewood, Lisa and Amy stood on the porches of their cabins, stretching and yawning.

"Morning, guys," the girls said at nearly the same time.

"Morning," the guys said, turning from the girls and heading into the woods.

"Want to go to the lake?" Amy asked Lisa.

"Sure! Let's go."

Lisa and Amy followed the trail outlined with rocks that lead to the lake. Jim and the other two guys had enough wood to cook and to last throughout the night. Lisa and Amy stripped naked and stood on the dock, but they seemed more interested in prancing up and down the dock than diving in. The three guys noticed them from the fire pit and decided to take a look.

"You think that they want us to see them?" Jon asked.

"I don't know, but I do know that those are some beautiful girls," Mike said.

As the three observed by the fire pit, a twig snapped in the woods. They quickly turned their attention toward the sound.

"You both see what I see?" Jim asked pointing toward the woods.

"Yes," the two answered. "It's Helen's son."

"John!" Jim called out. John quickly turned towards the three men, holding his dick in his hand.

Jon jumped up. "What the fuck are you doing, pervert?" he asked, walking fast towards the tree line.

John zipped up his pants and fled out of sight, pushing deeper into the woods. The girls had seen what happened, and they scrambled for their clothes, dressing themselves on the deck as fast as they could before rushing back to the fire pit.

"Who was that?" Lisa asked, out of breath.

"It was John Lewis," Jim said.

Mike laughed hard. "He saw you two naked in the lake and was beating his meat behind the tree there in the woods," he said. "Jim called his name and he ran off."

The boys joined in Mike's laughter, but the girls were visibly upset. Eventually, they decided to laugh it off as well, and volunteered to cook breakfast. The guys agreed. Jim started the fire using a small plastic jug of gasoline, while Jon and Mike placed the pots on the wooden benches. An agonized scream in the woods made everyone stop suddenly.

"Do we go and check on whoever that was?"   Amy asked.

"Jon," Jim said, "you stay here with the girls and help with the cooking,"

"Works for me," Jon replied.

Jim and Mike eased into the woods, scanning in all directions. Once they were deep enough into the woods that they couldn't see the campsite, Jim grabbed Mike by the shoulder. "Did you hear that?" he whispered.

"What?"

"Listen."

The two stood motionless. Someone was speaking not far away.

The two took careful steps until they could hear better, hiding themselves behind the fanned leaves of a huge palmetto bush. Peeking around the side of the bush on either side, they saw John Lewis on his knees, looking up at a huge man. As large as John was, this figure seemed to tower over him. Even from that distance, they judged this new man to be at least six and a half feet tall, and at least 250 lbs. He wore Navy blue khakis mottled with greenish gray moss ripped to tatters from the knees down, revealing mangled flesh and exposed bone on both legs. He wore a Navy blue long sleeve shirt, also encrusted with moss. The shirt was ripped as well, showing scarred and torn flesh that gave way to what appeared to be spots of exposed rib cage, bleached white from sun.   Long strands of stringy, greasy hair and greenish moss nearly obscured his hideous face, and the skin of his face looked bloodless and decayed.

"I beg of you, my son, do not kill me," John said on his knees. "I'm sorry for lusting against your mother."

The man raised a hatchet high overhead, and the dappled sunlight caught his worn, tan leather gloves.

"Please, my son! Please, Hatchetface!"

Hatchetface lowered the hatchet and clipped it onto a thick steel ring on his belt alongside long, wide metal files, and a hunting knife. A large leather pouch hung from his belt, just past the steel ring. He turned to look at Jim and Mike where they watched from the palmetto bush, then quickly pulled a 10" file with a wooden handle from his pouch. Before John could move, Hatchetface stabbed him through the temple. The file went through John's head and pierced the trunk of the tree beside him. Hatchetface turned his attention to Jim and Mike, but they were already running back towards the camp.

*   *   *

"We've got to go!" Jim yelled as soon as they made it back to the camp.

He searched his pants pockets until he found the Tahoe keys, pressed the unlock button on the keyless remote, and jumped in as Mike came up on the other side of the Tahoe and opened the passenger door.

At the firepit, Lisa stirred a pot of grits with a plastic ladle. "This better not be another joke!" she yelled. Jon and

Amy looked on, amused, but as Jim was getting in the Tahoe, Hatchetface walked up behind him.

"Who the hell are you, big fella?" Jon asked.

But Hatchetface did not respond. He pulled another 10" file from his leather belt and rammed it into Jim's skull, pinning him to the metal body of the Tahoe. With the passenger door still open, Mike stumbled backward, gawking. Standing much taller than the Tahoe, Hatchetface locked eyes with Mike, and Mike ran for the woods.

"Holy shit!" Amy screamed. She grabbed Lisa and Jon by the shoulders and almost tripped over one of the wooden benches.

Without a second thought, Jon pointed to the woods just as Mike crashed through the first few bushes before the underbrush grew thicker. "Go!" he yelled to the girls. "I'm right behind you!"

But Amy did not move. She stood frozen, watching blood pour from Jim's skull.

"Amy!" Jon yelled, almost to the woods. "Amy! Come on!"

She sputtered something, then turned and ran.

Hatchetface followed, walking at an easy gait.

*   *   *   *

Much farther ahead of the others, Mike circled back to the campsite. After waiting in the edge of the woods for a moment, he was satisfied that Hatchetface had gone. He rushed to Jim's lifeless body, twisted the file loose from the

Tahoe, then eased Jim's body to the grass. He found the keys under the Tahoe, started up the engine, and drove until he'd almost reached the dirt road, and looked back towards the camp one last time. As he turned his head forward to fix his eyes on the road once more, a hatchet smashed through the windshield and caught him in the forehead. Mike's foot slammed the gas pedal to the floorboard, and the Tahoe jumped the dirt road and came to a stop in the trees, steam boiling form under the crumpled hood.

CHAPTER FOUR

Jon, Amy, and Lisa squatted, huddled together in the brush.

"Listen girls," Jon said, "it'll be getting dark later and it looks like rain's coming in, so we need to get back to the camp, get some food in our bellies, and get our flashlights."

"What about that creature, or whatever the hell it is?" Amy asked.

"What about we fight him back?" Lisa asked.

"How?" Amy asked.

Jon reached behind him, raised his shirt tail, and pulled a 9mm pistol from the back of his jeans. He then aimed it toward the ground as his father had taught him, pulled back the slide, and made sure a bullet was in the chamber.

"Like this," Jon said.

"Where did you get that gun?" Amy asked.

"I told you I brought protection," Jon responded. "I'll lead us back to camp," Jon said as they all got to their feet.

  Back at the camp, they stopped between cabin #2 and cabin #3.

"You all see, or hear anything?" Amy asked softly.

"I see the fire is burnt down to ashes with very little smoke," Jon said, "and the Tahoe's gone."

"Where's Mike?" Lisa asked.

"That son of a bitch has left us stranded out here, I bet you," Jon said.

"Well, we have a gun, so come on," Lisa said.

The three stood by the fire pit.

"All right, Amy," Jon said. "you get a jug and fill it up with some kerosene. And get some matches."

"We're going to burn this mother?" Lisa asked.

"We have to try anything right now," Jon said.

Amy ran off towards the cabins, starting with hers and Lisa's.

"Now Lisa, you get a sheet and put the heaviest pots and pans in it, then tie it up."

"All right," Lisa said.

"Don't make it so heavy that you or Amy can't swing it, though," Jon said, heading back into the woods.

**   *

The three stood by the fire pit, looking around as Hatchetface stood between Cabins 2   and Cabin 3.

"There he is!" Amy exclaimed, pointing at the cabins.

"Let him come to us," Jon whispered

"So he's not a myth like Jim thought he was after all," Lisa said.

"Come on you motherfucker, come and get us!" Jon yelled standing at the fire pit with the pistol in his right hand.

Hatchetface walked towards them.

When Hacthetface was close enough that Jon knew he wouldn't miss, he aimed for a spot between Hatchetface's eyes and fired. Hatchetface staggered back two steps and fell on his back. Amy and Jon cautiously walked up to him. She opened the clear milk jug and dowsed the motionless body with kerosene before dropping the jug. She found the matches in the pocket of her jeans and struck one against the rough strip on the side of the matchbox. The heat of the flame pulsed through her finger and thumb, and she watched the flame for a moment, making sure it was full and ready before tossing it on the man, setting him on fire. As the two turned around towards Lisa standing at the fire pit, the creature sat up, blazing.

"Behind you!" Lisa yelled out.

Jon turned, quickly raising the gun. When he fired it made him lose his balance, but he didn't fall. The rain had begun to fall heavy and it put out the fire which burned the creature. Jon dropped the 9mm pistol to the ground because it had no more bullets, nor did he have another clip. Lisa picked up the sheet from the ground with pots and swung it hitting the creature in the upper body; she then uppercut the creature with her right hand knocking him down again. Lisa turned and ran down the path after dropping the sheet. Jon ran into the woods behind the outhouse, and Amy ran down to the dock. The creature got up on his feet again and heard Jon calling for Amy. Jon came out from behind the outhouse onto the trail for Amy to see him from the dock. Hatchetface walked behind the cabins and grabbed his hunting knife from his sheath then threw it hitting Jon in the cheeks of his mouth. The knife went through both sides of his mouth. Hatchetface walked towards Jon on his knees now on the trail. He stood behind Jon and grabbed the knife by the handle, and blade. He then pulled back, then up cutting Jon's head in half. Amy screamed from the dock and ran into the woods. Jon's body fell limply to the ground as he was killed on his knees.

Lisa tried to spot her sister in the woods, but she could not.

Hatchetface did not run toward Lisa.

Amy was running eastward in the swamp as fast as she could in mud Hatchetface hiding behind a large cypress tree when she passed by. He sliced her across her abdomen. She ran another ten feet then stopped and looked back to see Hatchetface. She then put both hands on her abdomen as the slice opened up and her guts fell into her hands.

*   *   *

Back on the dirt road, Lisa ran.   "Four or five more miles to go before I'm back at the Lewis house," she thought. She ran, panting in the heat until she could run no more. Walking now that her lungs and legs burned, she ran her sandpaper tongue along the roof of her mouth.

CHAPTER FIVE

As dusk covered the earth, Lisa saw headlights coming towards her. She flagged down the gold Town and Country Van, and it came to a stop beside her. The driver let his window down.

"What are you doing out here, girl?" he asked.

"My friends and I were camping," she stammered, pointing back down the road.

"Down at Camp Okefenokee?" the driver asked. He furrowed his brow and tilted his head, waiting for her answer.

"Yes."

"Well hell, that's where we're headed. I'm Kevin. Pleased to meet you."

"No! Please don't go!" Lisa begged.

"Are your friends still down there?" the driver asked.

"No, they're dead. All dead."

The driver readjusted his ball cap so that Lisa could see his face. He was young, most likely in his early twenties, with a chaw of tobacco snug in his cheek. His stubble stood out in glow of the van's instrument cluster.

"Dead?" he said. "What happened?"

"This big guy showed up out of nowhere and--"

"Did you call the law?"

"I lost my phone."

"What'd he look like?"

"He wore all blue and had these gloves. He killed one of my friends with this long file or something."

The driver slapped the steering wheel and laughed. "Shit," he said, "you almost had me with that old Hatchetface story."

"He's real! I swear!"

"I thought you looked crazy before, but you're just fucked up, ain't you?"

"Fucked up," Lisa mumbled, then mouthed the words. "No. I'm not on anything. I'm telling the truth. I know it sounds crazy, but--"

"He killed all your friends, huh?"

"Well, I don't know if he got my sister. Please, you have to call the police."

"And tell 'em what? A kid's ghost story killed your friends? Not hardly. So are you getting in or not? I ain't got all night, tweaker."

"No. You couldn't pay me to go back there." As she turned to continue walking, an image of her sister flashed through her mind. She saw her hiding in the woods, alone, scared, hunted, wondering why

"Aww, come one. We can help you rescue your sister," said someone from the passenger's seat.

"How many of you are in there?" Lisa asked.

"Four. Two boys and two girls," the driver responded.

"What do you have for protection?" Lisa asked.

"A whole box of condoms," the driver responded, laughing, and the other passengers joined in.

Thunder rolled, and lightning flashed in the southern sky.

"Are you coming or not? It's getting dark?" the driver said.

"All right, okay," Lisa said. "I'll go. And I'm not on drugs." She opened the sliding door and got into the van.

"Then you're no fun," one of the girls teased as she slid over to make room for Lisa.

*   *   *

"Well, here we are," Kevin said shutting off the engine.

"It's dark out here," Lisa said.

Everyone got out.

"Wait a second, how rude are we?" the driver asked. "This here is Ken Waters, and these wild things are Stacy and Lacy Hill."

"Lisa Sparks," Lisa said, already scanning what she could see of the tree line.

"Okay then," Kevin said, shining the flashlight on the other four. "Now that we got the introductions done and over with, let's find our cabins and wait until this storm passes."

Ken walked over to Cabin 1 and looked for a lamp, lantern, or some type of lighting. "Fuck," he said, "looks like we'll be sleeping in the dark tonight until we can go back to town tomorrow and get some battery lanterns or something."

"I might have another flashlight in the glove compartment," Kevin said.

"I'll check on it," Ken said walking towards the van.

"We shouldn't be out here you guys," Lisa said.

Kevin shined the flashlight in her face, and she turned her head. He smirked. "Nothing's going to happen here, Lisa. Trust me."

"I know," Lisa muttered under her breath. "It's already begun."

"What's that?" Lacy asked Lisa.

"They'll just think I'm crazy," Lisa thought. But she smiled and replied, "Oh, nothing. I just talk to myself when I get nervous around new people."

"Aww, sugar," Stacy chimed in, "no need to be nervous around us!"

"I got another flashlight," Ken said as he held two flashlights in his hands.

"Give it to Lisa, then," Kevin said.

Ken walked over to Lisa and handed her the flashlight. "Guys and girls," he said, "Stacy and me are going to Cabin 1."

"Me and Lacy will take Cabin 2, then," Kevin said.

"I'll take Cabin 3, then," Lisa said. "It's not like I'm really going to sleep anyways," she muttered.

*   *   *

Rain pummeled the tin roof as Lisa sat on the bed in the dark, thinking of how to find her sister. A streak of jagged lightning flashed through the tiny cabin window, and a boom of thunder sounded just after.

In Ken and Stacy's cabin, the flash of lightning illuminated Ken's face as he shut his eyes. Stacy straddled him, and Ken reached up to grab hold of her breasts while she held her long black hair up on top of her head, moaning and writhing. But once the lightning had passed, the cabin went dark.

Neither of them heard the cabin door squeak open, nor did they see Hatchetface as he stepped inside and eased his hunting knife from its sheath. He stood beside them for a moment, accustomed to the darkness of the swamp, gauging where they were in bed by the sounds they made. "I'm coming," Stacy said in a low whisper.

"That's right," Ken urged, "come for me."

Hatchetface plunged his knife into Stacy's throat, spraying the bed and Ken's eyes with her hot blood as the knife up through her neck until the blade caught her jawbone. Hatchetface pulled out the knife, and Stacy fell forward onto Ken, spasming. Ken pushed at Stacy's still-warm corpse with one hand and grabbed at his eyes with the other. "Kevin!" he yelled as Stacy's body hit the floor. He jumped up, stumbling in the dark.   "Kevin!" he yelled again. "Somebody help me!"

Like an animal savoring the moment before a kill, Hatchetface stood back, sensing where Ken stood by the smell of Stacy's blood and sound of his hand feeling along the wall. Ken was about to scream for help once more, but as he opened his mouth Hatchetface sliced through the corners of his mouth. Ken fell to the floor, crawling now, and Hatchetface followed, taking his time as Ken drug himself down the cabin steps face-first, groaning. Hatchetface followed him to the fire pit. In their cabin, Kevin and Lacy laughed, oblivious to what was happening just outside. Hatchetface put his knife away in its sheath and picked up one of the rocks that circled the fire pit. Placing his wide foot between Ken's shoulders, he pressed his face to the ground. "Please," Ken whimpered.   Hatchetface dropped the rock on Ken's head, bursting out his eyes and brain. Blood poured from his nose and mouth and mixed with the muddy earth, but Hatchetface did not concern himself with this. He had already turned his attention to Cabin 2.

CHAPTER SIX

"I've got to pee Kevin," Lacy said.

"Right when it's getting good," Kevin said.

"I have an overactive bladder, okay?"

Lacy snatched on her pajama pants and shirt, then hurried down the warped wooden steps of the cabin. She was already several yards away when she patted the pocket of her pajama pants. "Damn," she said. "Forgot the flashlight." She squinted in the rain and darkness until another flash of lightning showed her the silhouette of the outhouse at the edge of the woods, and she ran toward it, fixing the image in her mind.

When she'd finished, she stepped out of the outhouse and held the door with her left hand, waiting for another flash of lightning to show her the way. She stretched her free arm high in an attempt to pull her mated, wet hair from her eyes as Hatchetface came out from behind the outhouse and sliced into her midsection with his hatchet, cutting her in half. Her separated body lay in front of the outhouse as thunder rolled and lightning flashed.

After several minutes had passed, Kevin sat up in bed. "Where is she?" he said.

He got out of bed and took up his flashlight from the nightstand. He stood on the porch of the cabin and called out Lacy's name. Lisa heard him and walked onto the porch of her cabin, but Kevin couldn't see her in the dark.

"Lacy!" Kevin called out again.

For a moment, Lisa thought of telling him to stop shouting. She opened her mouth, about to tell him it was no use, but she stopped herself. None of them would heed her warnings. As quietly as she could manage, she slipped back inside her cabin and locked the door. She heard Kevin slopping his way to the outhouse, determined to let him meet his fate. *"Dammit,"* she thought, *"he doesn't have any idea what he's dealing with."* Without any further hesitation, she grabbed her flashlight and unlocked the cabin door.

Lisa had her flashlight in her right hand and she went down her cabin's steps, unsure of where Kevin had gone. She passed Cabin 2 and went up Cabin 1's steps, keeping her flashlight off until she needed it. At the door to Cabin 1, her flashlight's beam showed her the patterns of blood smeared on the white bed sheets, as well as the fine spray of blood on the floor and walls of the cabin. She ran out of the cabin, heading towards the van, and as she ran, she swung her flashlight, sending a yellow beam of light careening from the trees then down to the ground, then back again. Kevin saw the light and yelled out to her as he stood at the outhouse, but she did not look back. She rifled through the van, but when she could not find the keys, she used her flashlight to find the road.

"Where you going?" Kevin called. "Fucking tweaker," he said to himself, bare feet squishing in the soggy grass as he neared the outhouse. He opened the door, but the outhouse was empty.

He shut the door and stepped back, catching Hatchetface in his light.

"Holy shit!" Kevin yelled, looking up at the impossibly tall man.

Hatchetface pressed his hatchet into Kevin's chest and sliced downward. A gust of wind blew back Kevin's shirt, exposing his ribs and organs. Kevin dropped his flashlight and grasped his stomach with both hands, trying to keep his insides from falling out, but Hatchetface raised the hatchet and severed his arms at the shoulders. Kevin's screams pierced through the sound of the rain beating against the forest canopy and the hollow ping of the raindrops on the tin roofs of the cabins.

Kevin dropped to his knees, then fell forward.

Hatchetface put his hatchet away in the metal ring of his tool belt. With a low grunt, he took Kevin by his ankles, holding them together in one hand. He held him up in this manner, and shook him, but his organs did not fall out. Displeased, Hatchetface whipped Kevin's corpse against the outhouse. A string of innards fell out in the grass and mud, and some of it spattered the side of the outhouse. Hatchetface did this again and again until nothing came out of the body, then dropped it and turned back toward the cabins.

She had stopped running now to get her breathe. She was now speed walking and was close to where Kevin and the others had picked her up at earlier. But she knew that no

place was safe, not even four miles away at Helen's, but that

was her destination.

ERNEST ROBERSON SR-

CHAPTER SEVEN

Lisa knocked on the door of the Lewis house three times then stepped back, letting the screen door swing shut. She turned to face the road, about the switch on her flashlight when she heard, "Yes, dear?" from behind her.

Helen stood in the doorway, a look of concern on her face.

"You startled me," Lisa said.

"Well, are you coming in or are you going to stand out there and talk with me through the screen door?" Helen asked.

Helen led the way with her lantern. Lisa shut the door and took the love seat, while Helen sat in her chair and set the lantern on the wooden end table beside her, casting the living room in a pale shade of orange that shifted and danced. "So what is it that I may do for you dear?" Helen asked.

"What more can you tell me about Hatchetface?"

"Well, one year ago, give or take, some kids ranging from 17 to 19 picked this boy up walking down this dirt road. They took him on to the camp with them. And there they took him snipe hunting. So he was mangled by the alligators, panthers, snakes, and even a bear. The wounds that the animals inflicted killed him."

"No," Lisa said, looking Helen in the eye. "Not the ghost story. The real thing."

Helen grinned for the first time since Lisa has met her.

"I take it you know he's not just a myth?" Helen said.

"I know you have something to do with this. Who is he?"

"John Lewis, Jr. is his name, dear. 'Hatchetface' sounds so gruesome. Hardly the name I'd have wished on him. But you can't help what people want to call your son. That's one of the burdens of being a mother."

"Your son?"

"Yes," Helen said. "Such a sweet, sweet boy. But now? I can't say."

"You have to stop him! Helen, he's killed people! He killed all my friends."

"And that's my fault? Am I to take my own son's life? I don't think so. Besides, he's not...he's not the same now."

"When will your husband be home?" Lisa asked, looking toward the door.

Helen chuckled. "Now why would you want to see my husband?"

"I need him to get me out of here!"

"I haven't seen him in nearly a day now," Helen said. "He can't be gone too far, though. His wrecker is out there in the yard."

"Well, how did Hatchetface get his name?" Lisa asked.

Helen once again grinned.

"After the kids done what they done, dawn had broken, and they hadn't seen John. So they went back into the swamp where they left him and seen a horrible body. My boy was mangled and mauled up. So John, Sr. and me buried at Camp Okefenokee Cemetery, behind the outhouse and cabins. And whenever everyone left, so did John, Sr. and me. But then John Sr. went back and placed some old files, a hunting knife, and a hatchet on the grave. They were some of his favorite things, being an outdoorsman as he was. Call it superstition or being an old sentimental man, but John, Sr. thought it would be a nice gesture. A couple days later we went back to the grave and everything was gone.

Now that's about all I can tell, because that's all that I know."

"Do you mind if I rest here tonight, and I'll walk to town in the morning?" Lisa asked.

"I don't mind one bit dear," Helen said getting up from her rocking chair. "I'll get you a blanket.

Lisa laid on the brown couch with her shoes still on and Helen covered her up with a wool blanket. Helen turned the lantern down low and fell asleep herself in her chair.

Outside, lightning flashed once. The blast of white light caught Hatchetface as he stood on the porch.

*   *   *

The third day came without fail. Lisa woke up after a good rested night on Helen's couch. She pulled the wool blanket off of her, got to her feet and folded the blanket up to put it on the couch.

"You didn't have to do that dear, and good morning," Helen said from her chair.

Lisa sat back on the couch and rubbed her eyes.

"You know maybe I'll make it home today," Lisa said removing her hands from her face.

Helen grinned, then said to Lisa,

"Once you come here, you never really get to leave. You seemed like a smart girl. I thought you'd have figured it out by now."

"What does that mean?" Lisa asked.

"He won't let you leave the cursed land," Helen replied.

"Watch me then," Lisa said. She got up off of the couch and looked at Helen. "Goodbye, Helen. I'm sorry he didn't kill me, too. I know that pissed you off, you crazy old bitch."

Helen only grinned as Lisa walked towards the front door and opened it. Never looking back she went out of the doorway and closed it back shut. Lisa let the screen door free of her right hand, but did not hear it slap shut behind her. She stopped, turned, and saw a long wood-file lodged in the front door, keeping the screen door open. Lisa turned back towards the driveway and walked towards the dirt road.

Once she made it to the muddy red clay dirt road she went left going towards Highway 177.

"Four miles," Lisa said, in a normal tone aloud.

As she walked, she looked behind herself every few minutes, checking the woods that surrounded her on either side. Lisa heard something to her left that startled her, so she began running. As she ran she looked around herself in all directions, then in front of her. In the distance she saw cars on Highway 177. All she needed to do was make it another 200 yards.

But when she looked behind her, she saw Hatchetface walking down the the middle of the muddy clay road, hatchet drawn. He did not seem to be in any hurry.

A green F-150 barreled down the highway. Its low-beam lights cast a soft glow in the morning fog seeping off the asphalt as the sun warmed 177 South. Lisa stood with one foot on each side of the double-yellow lines in the middle of the highway, then jumped up and down, yelling and waving her arms. The F-150 slowed and parked on the shoulder of the road. The driver rolled down his window.

"Hello miss," he said. He was an older man, with thinning hair and a thick grey mustache. "Are you all right?" He hung one elbow out of the open window, and the drizzling rain beaded on the sleeve of his nylon jacket.

"Get me the hell out of here!" Lisa said, already running around to the passenger's side. She pulled on the handle, but it would not open. She looked through the window. "Please!" she said. "I'm not crazy! I just need to get out of here! Somebody's following me."

"Who?" the man asked. He squinted at Lisa. She hadn't stopped to think about it, but she realized she probably looked deranged. She hadn't had a shower in two days, and red clay clung to her shoes and weighed down the cuffs of her jeans.

"Please," she begged, "I can explain later. Just get me out of here!"

"You probably wouldn't believe me even if I told you," Lisa said.

The man nodded, then the passenger door clicked, and Lisa jumped inside and slammed the door.

"I'm Rodney Seabolt by the way," he said. "What's your name?"

"Lisa," she said, staring ahead. "Can we go now?"

"Sure." Rodney put the truck in drive and began to drive away, but Lisa looked back. She saw only the dirt road.

*   *   *

Rodney stopped the truck at the stop sign then turned left onto US-1 north.

"So where are you headed?" Rodney asked.

"How far can you take me?" Lisa asked.

"Well I'm off work, but I'm in a government truck. Not my personal one."

"Government truck?"

"I'm a game warden. Sounds like of somebody's chasing you, it'd be best to speak with the police."

"I lost my phone," Lisa said, watching the houses and farmland fly past. She wanted Rodney to drive faster. She wanted to tell him everything that happened, but she did not. Who would believe her? "Do you have one?" she asked. "I need to call my parents."

Rodney pulled a flip phone from his shirt pocket and passed it to her.

"Damn it," Lisa said, giving the phone back to Rodney.

"No one home?"

Lisa did not respond.

"Listen," Rodney said, "I'm not a cop, but I have some friends in Waycross at the Sheriff Department. Do you want to go there?" Rodney asked.

"Why not?" Lisa said. "Maybe he'll follow me there, and the whole police department will see him."

"See who? I mean, that's your business, but the police won't be able to help you if you don't tell them what's going on."

"You think I'm just some crazy girl, don't you?"

Rodney shook his head and lifted one hand from the steering wheel, gesturing toward the roof of the truck. "I don't know what to think, missy. Why don't you try me?"

Lisa kicked off her shoes and drew her knees up to her chest. "Okay. But before I tell you, I want you to know I'm not drunk, and I'm not on drugs. Everything I'm going to say is true."

"I'm listening."

Lisa let out a sigh, then said, "I was with my friends out at Camp Okefenokee. Some man showed up out of the swamp and murdered them. I think he killed my sister, but I'm not sure."

"What did he look like?"

"Promise you won't laugh?"

"Promise."

"He was really tall, and he was wearing all blue, ripped up clothes, and gloves. He used a hatchet, and these long wood-files--"

"You mean Hatchetface?"

Lisa was silent for a moment, then said, "Yes," in a quiet voice before staring out of the passenger window."

"Huh. Well, that's a hard pill to swallow, Lisa. But if that's what you say happened, I'll believe you. If your story checks out, I'll get some other wardens and deputies together and head out there." Rain began to fall on the windshield. "If what you're saying is true, then there should be plenty of evidence."

"There is," Lisa said. She turned toward Rodney and put her hand on his shoulder. "If you look in those cabins, there'll be blood everywhere. I can go with you and show you everything."

Rodney looked down at Lisa's hand, and she removed it. "Sorry," she said, "but you're the first person who's believed me at all. Just go up to the Lewis house and talk with Helen. She knows everything. She might not tell you, but she knows."

"Let's not get ahead of ourselves, missy," said Rodney. "You just rest, and get it all straight in your head. Like I said, you need to be calm when you tell them about this, or they'll think you're playing a prank. You wouldn't believe how many calls we get about Hatchetface."

"So why do you believe me?"

"I didn't say I believed the part about Hatchetface," Rodney said, "but it's obvious something bad happened to you out there in the swamp. Just rest. We'll be there soon."

Lisa put her head against the passenger side window and shut her eyes, listening to the low hum of the truck's engine and the soft nasal croon of some long-dead country singer on the radio.

CHAPTER EIGHT

"We're here," Rodney said.

Lisa woke up. The building's low, long brickwork reminded Lisa of her high-school. It looked safe, impenetrable.

Inside, deputies manned phones and computers at their desks. A group of officers stood in front of a gridded map of the county, determining a radius around a red dot they'd marked. The fluorescent lights caught the handles of the pistols strapped to their hips. She'd expected that this would make her feel more protected, but she remembered how Hatchetface had all but laughed as Jon shot him again and again. To try and take her mind off of this, she made it a point to focus on what was happening in the present moment. Rodney was leaning on a desk, speaking with a deputy, and she read the name "Randall Hood" engraved on his name tag.

"Anyway, is the sheriff in?" Rodney asked.

"What's this about?" Randall asked, shifting in his chair.

"Something pretty serious, I'm afraid."

Randall took on a serious expression. "Oh," he said. "Hold on a second." He picked up his phone. "Sherriff hate to bother you, but Rodney Seabolt is here. He says it's something serious. Okay. I'll tell him." He hung up the phone. "He'll be out in just a minute. Y'all can have a seat. Can I get you some coffee?"

"No, thanks," Lisa said. "And I'd rather stand, if you don't mind."

Randall nodded. "Suit yourself."

The sheriff came out after a few minutes. "Rodney," he said. "Good to see you, brother. What can I do for you?"

Rodney shook hands with the sheriff. "Wayne," Rodney said, "this is Lisa."

Lisa stepped up and shook hands. "Lisa Sparks," she said.

"Wayne Selph. Pleased to meet you. Y'all can come on back."

As Rodney and Lisa began to follow the sheriff down the long hallway, something shattered behind them. They turned to see a hatchet buried deep in the chest of a deputy as he sat at his desk. He gurgled blood and fell out of his chair.

"He's here!" Lisa screamed.

Rodney reached inside his jacket and drew a pistol from his shoulder holster. "Go!" he said. Several officers jumped to their feet, guns drawn, flanking Rodney. All of them watched, dumbfounded, as Hatchetface kicked in the first set of metal doors. He glared at them through the shattered glass of the second set of doors and grinned.

"Rodney," the sheriff asked, "what the hell is this?"

Lisa hid her face in the sheriff's chest, crying. "It's Hatchetface!" she sobbed. "He's come for me!"

A young deputy came up beside the sheriff, pistol drawn. "You mean, that shit's for real?"

"Looks real enough to me," Rodney said.

Hatchetface took a step back, then kicked in the remaining set of doors--the only barrier between him and the officers.

The officers fired in unison, but Hatchetface simply grunted, as if he were a heavyweight boxer play-fighting with a child. He lunged through the hail of bullets and, with one huge hand, grabbed Rodney's pistol and wrist. The officers jumped back, some of them still firing while others reloaded. Hatchetface snatched Rodney's arm downward with such force that the Ulna bone jutted through the skin, then pulled the bone free and rammed it into Rodney's neck before casting him to the tile floor.

The sheriff fired his pistol until the slide kicked back, telling him it was time to reload. "Come with me," he whispered. As the other officers continued firing, Lisa ran behind the sheriff down a long hallway, and she noticed that he was on his phone. He hung up and pulled her down a side hall that ended in an emergency exit. "Go down Main Street to First Avenue," he said, out of breath. "You'll meet my daughter at the corner there. She works at the diner."

"I don't understand," Lisa said over the blaring gunshots down the hall.

"Go out the back door there," Wayne said, pointing.

"Then go to your right and take the first alley to the right, at the end of that is Main Street, then go left," Wayne said.

"Why are you sending me to your daughter?"

"She'll explain. If we can't take him down, she's the only hope you've got. Now go!"

"Thank you," Lisa said as Wayne opened the door, sounding the alarm.

Back down the hallway, Randall stood closest to Hatchetface, firing his pistol. Hatchetface grabbed the gun out of his hands and jammed it into Randall's mouth, shattering his teeth and breaking his jawbone. Hatchetface pulled his hunting knife from its sheath and slit Randall's throat to reveal the barrel of the pistol lodged in his throat as

he fell to the floor.

A deputy came running from a side-office, holding

the stock of his 12-gauge pump shotgun tight against his

shoulder as he blasted Hatchetface again and again, kicking

still-smoking shells out onto the floor. When he ran out of

shells, Hatchetface grabbed the shotgun from him, flipped it

around backward, and ran him through with the barrel.

Wayne had made it back down the hallway.

Hatchetface turned to face him, surrounded by still-bleeding,

mangled bodies. Wayne was the only one left. He took aim

with his .38 revolver, and said, "Come one, you motherfu--"

Before he could finish his sentence, Hatchetface drew a 10"

wood-file and jammed it through his head, punching

through his jaw and sticking out of the top of his skull.

Hatchetface held him up by the file's handle, then dropped

him. He pulled his file out of Wayne's skull, retrieved his

hatchet, and followed the long hallway as the alarm wailed.

ERNEST ROBERSON SR-

ERNEST ROBERSON SR-

CHAPTER NINE

Lisa bent over, hands on her knees, struggling to catch her breath. She'd made it to First Avenue, out front of Maggie's Diner. A black rag top Mustang pulled up beside her. The driver rolled down the passenger window. She was a young brunette, with her hair pulled up in a ponytail. "You Lisa?" she asked.

"Yeah," Lisa huffed. "Are you the sheriff's daughter?"

"That's me. Get in"

Lisa got in, and Tina sped away. "He's in the city?" Tina asked.

"Yeah, I just came from the sheriff's office."

Tina clinched one of her hands into a fist and beat the steering wheel. "Goddammit," she said. "Daddy…"

"He might've made it."

"No," Tina said, wiping at her eyes. "Nobody makes it. Well, almost nobody."

"So you know he's real?"

"You have no idea," Tina said with a tear streaked face.

"What do you mean?"

"I'm one of the four people who played the snipe hunting game on him. Me and my boyfriend thought it'd be funny to send him off in the woods while we had sex. The other couple played along with it, too."

"So you're the only survivor from that night?" Lisa asked.

"No. My boyfriend John made it, too. has nothing to do with me or our baby, Susan Selph. I named her that because I couldn't name her after him." Tina said.

"So can your boyfriend help?"

"I'm not with him anymore. I got pregnant that night, and now he doesn't want anything to do with me or Susan."

"What about the other two? What happened to them?"

"Mary and her husband Carlos, yeah. They went to John Lewis, Jr.'s funeral. Then they went back out there again, I guess because they felt guilty. That's when they vanished."

"What should we do?" Lisa asked. "Your dad said you'd know what to do."

"Shit," she said, "I don't know. I told him about Hatchetface, but he thought I was just trying to distract him from the fact that I'd gotten knocked-up. We were never on the best of terms."

Lisa gripped the Mustang's dash. "So we don't have a plan?"

"All I now to do is go to see if John will help."

"What if we call the law?"

"And tell them what? Some superhuman swamp zombie that I helped create is on the loose? They'll have us both in straitjackets by morning."

"How can John help?" Lisa asked.

"You know Helen, right? Crazy old bat."

"Yeah. What about her?"

"I talked with her about it a few times. She said it had something to do with old Indian magic or some shit. Said since he died the way he did, he'll keep killing until he's laid to rest."

"I don't trust her," Lisa said. "Hatchetface is her son. Why would she help us kill him?"

"It's all we've got to go on. I don't believe in all that mumbo jumbo bullshit, but if that's what made him, that's what can stop him. Since me and John were responsible for his death, and the other two are dead, maybe we're the only ones that can fix this. I'd hoped he'd just fade away so we could live normal lives. But then my dad kept getting calls about Hatchetface. Of course, he thought they were all prank calls, but he investigated one of them. Couldn't find anything, but he knew something was up."

"Does John believe Hatchetface is real?"

"He says he doesn't, but I know he does. It's all I know to do."

Tina drove on, heading towards Hoboken.

*　　*　　*

Tina and pulled into a gravel driveway which circled around the front yard of a beige double wide. Halfway around the driveway, Tina stopped the car and put it in park.

"You coming?" Tina asked.

Lisa followed Tina onto the front screened in porch. Tina knocked on the door until a tall, man in his mid-twenties opened the door.

"John," Tina said.

"What the fuck are you doing here?"

"We need to talk," Tina said.

"About Susan?" John asked. He looked over at Lisa. "Who's this?" he asked.

"No, Susan's fine, no thanks to you," Tina said.

"I'm Lisa. We need your help."

"Help?"

Tina put one hand on her hip. "Just let us in, asshole."

"Well, if you're gonna be so nice about it, come on in," John said.

John sat in a dark blue recliner. Lisa and Tina sat on a black couch that looked as though it had been clawed and chewed by a large dog.

"Looks like you're living the high life, now," Tina scoffed.

"Fuck you, bitch," John hissed. "What do you want?"

Tina leaned forward and looked John in the eye. "He's killing again," she said. "We need you to help us stop him."

"He who?" John asked.

"Hatchetface."

John threw his hands up and laughed. "Aww, shit," he said, laughing. "Here we go again."

"You know he's real," Tina said, her voice stern and serious. "Please, John. I haven't asked you for anything since you left. But I need you now."

For a moment, John smiled. But the longer he held Tina's gaze, the more serious his expression grew. "He killed those cousins, Tina," he said, his voice soft and scared. "Carved them up like he was doing it for fun.

"Cousins?" Lisa asked.

John nodded and looked at Lisa. "They were with us. It was me, Tina, Mary, Carlos, and the two cousins. You can count me out."

"We have to," Tina said. "We started this, and we have to end it."

"All based on what? Some old bitch's hocus pocus story?"

"You tell me, John. Hatchetface isn't human, at least not anymore. If we did something that created him, then we can stop him."

"Call the law," John said.

"They won't help us," Tina snapped, but then she looked at the floor. "He killed my daddy."

"Holy shit," John said, rubbing his eyes. "He went into the city?"

"Yes. I'm sure they'll write it up as some deranged killer that hated cops, but they won't stop him. Nobody knows he's real but us."

"What does she have anything to do with this?" John asked pointing towards Lisa from the recliner.

Everyone got quiet as a door opened down the hallway of the trailer.

"Baby, who's here?" a girl's voice asked.

A thin, young blonde walked out of the hallway, looked into the living room and into the kitchen. She wore only a white dress shirt, and she pulled it close and crossed her arms as she stood in the kitchen, looking over the bar and into the living room.

"Carla," John said, "this is Tina and Lisa."

"What's that slut doing in our house?" Carla said.

John jumped up from the recliner and walked to a corner where he could see into the kitchen and the living room.

"I've got to go somewhere, Carla. It's an emergency"

"Where John, to bed with these whores?

"I'm no whore," Lisa insisted.

"If you associate with that bitch, you must be," Carla snapped. "I'm enough for you, John. You know it."

"Listen damn it, we don't have time for this stupid shit," Lisa said as she stood. "We need to go."

"You're welcome to come with us, baby," John said. "We're going to do something important, and we may need you."

Carla dashed out of the kitchen, into a bedroom, and slammed the door. John looked in the living room at the two girls standing and then followed after Carla. After ten minutes, John and John walked into the living room with a suitcase in his hand as Carla followed, fully dressed. John put the suitcase by the recliner and sat as Carla sat on the arm of the recliner.

"Look," Carla said, "I don't like either of you, but if it's important to John, its important to me. He told me what's up. I think you're all crazy, but I'm tagging along to make sure y'all don't get yourselves killed."

"Now that we're all in agreement that this is absolutely fucking insane" John said, "what's the plan? You do have one, don't you?"

"We have to put him back into his grave, his final resting spot," Tina replied.

"Sounds good, it really does," John said sarcastically, "but what all do we need to do that?"

"Food, firewood, and maybe even some gasoline," Tina said.

"We need kerosene for the lanterns," Lisa said. "We used it to burn him."

"How'd that work out?" John asked.

"It slowed him down some," Lisa replied.

"Shit," John said, rubbing the back of his head. "We're up against an undead monster that just slaughtered a half of Ware County's police force, and all we got are three girls, me, some gas and kerosene. Sounds about right." He stood from the recliner. "All right, we'll take my truck. I got some blocks of wood already cut up under the shelter out back. We can load them up in the back. I'll get the tarp to keep them dry. I got some jugs, and we can stop on the way and get the gas and kerosene."

"I'll bring some food," Carla said opening up the pantry door in the kitchen. "Y'all are going to work up an appetite killing monsters."

They loaded the truck, and John turned on the ignition. Everyone then got into the truck, but John went back inside. When he came back out, he had a green metal ammo box in his left hand and a crossbow in his right hand. He placed the ammo box and crossbow in the back of the truck beside the empty kerosene and gas jugs, pulled the black tarp across the truck's bed, and tied down the corners.

He hopped up in the F-250 and shut the door.

"What's this?" Lisa said, sitting in the back. She held up a metal bat. "You play baseball?"

"That's a softball bat, girl," John said. "Never know when you might run across some undesirables."

"Yeah," Tina said, "or somebody's husband."

ERNEST ROBERSON SR-

CHAPTER TEN

The clouds vanished, and the sun beamed down. John filled two lanterns for cabins 2 and 3 with kerosene and placed blocks of wood by the fire pit for the night. Carla put the suitcase in Cabin 2. The four sat on the wooden benches around the fire pit.

A mosquito buzzed by Carla's face, and she swatted at it. "It's so muggy," she said.

"Not a fan of the outdoors, are you, Carla?" Tina laughed.

"You all hear that?" John asked, looking at the tree tops.

"Hear what?" Carla asked looking also into the blue sky.

"Nature," John replied. "Birds, bugs chirping, and such. I've done my part, girls. What's the rest of the plan?"

"If the burial grounds are his final resting place," Lisa said, "maybe we head down there?"

"Maybe," John said. "Sounds like the blind leading the blind."

"If y'all gets your asses killed out here," Carla said, swatting at another mosquito, "it won't be my fault."

John opened pulled the ammo box closer to him on the wooden bench and opened it. He reached inside, pulled out a nickel-plated .357 revolver, and kicked out the cylinder, checking to see that the gun was not loaded. He reached into the box once again and grabbed a hand full of hollow point bullets. He stood and put the shells in the pocket of his jeans and held the pistol by his side.

"Ready?" John asked, closing the ammo box.

Tina walked on the trail outlined with rocks by the outhouse as the other three followed. She and the other three had walked nearly one-hundred yards past the outhouse when they spotted headstones, statues of angels, crosses, and flat stone slabs.

"Be careful where you walk," Tina said, still leading the way.

Just after Tina had spoken those words, Carla's left leg sunk into a grave up to her knee. She screamed as John pulled her out of it.

"Look," Tina said, pointing ahead. "There it is!"

The grave was five feet above ground level. The four surrounded it, standing at each corner. The solid concrete top rose to waist-height, covered with greenish moss, but the center of the concrete slab had been broken from the inside. An angel statue, also covered with green-yellow moss, prayed over the grave.

*　　　*　　　*

As the four sat around the fire pit on the wooden benches they wondered what they to do now that the rain and clouds have moved out.

"He'll be here any minute," Lisa said.

"I doubt it," Tina replied. "He'll wait until nightfall. That's how he operates."

"But he hit the sheriff's office in broad daylight," Lisa said.

"He was chasing you," Tina retorted. "Now that we're back on his home turf, he'll take it slow, wait until we drop our guard probably."

"So you're an expert on him now, that it?" John snorted.

"No, I just mean that's what he'd normally do."

"Fuck that," Carla said. "I'm going swimming. Let me know when he gets here." She walked down to the dock.

"We need to stay together!" Lisa called after her.

"Let her go," John said. "She's stubborn as hell. Almost as stubborn as Tina."

Tina rolled her eyes. "I am *nothing* like that trash."

"John, if you'll start the fire we'll cook," Lisa said.

John stacked some wood in the fire pit, poured some gasoline on the logs, and lit it with a match. He then went and got some pots and cooking utensils out of the bed of the truck, and Tina and Lisa brought the food from the truck. As the girls cooked, John walked down to the dock, where

Carla splashed around in her highlighter pink bra and panties.

Standing on the end of the dock, John looked down at her. "How's the water?" he asked

"Wet," Carla said, with a grin and pulled herself up onto the dock.

She sat with one leg stretched out on the dock but left the other in the water as she faced the camp.

"Is this all a big joke or something?" Carla asked. "You can't really expect me to believe this shit about Hatchetface."

"Tina and me have some unfinished business out here," John explained still standing, looking out at the lake.

"Well," Carla said, rubbing herself through her panties, "as long as you're not fucking her anymore, I don't care what you do." She laid back into the water once more, barely making a splash. She came up from underneath the water and brushed her hair backward with her hands. "You coming in or not?" she asked, treading water.

"Fuck it," John said. He stripped down to his blue boxers and dove in head-first.

When he came up, he spewed water in Carla's face.

"You asshole!" she said, and slapped water at him playfully.

"It is nice out here, isn't it?"

Carla grinned. "Come on over here and I'll show you something even better." She swam out toward the middle of the lake, and John let her go, feigning disinterest. "Oh, come on," she yelled across the water, "don't make me start without you!"

Cupping his hands, John cut through the water, taking his time. When he was about ten feet from her, Carla ducked under the surface, then popped back up.

"You silly girl," John said. "Trying to play lifeguard?" But then he saw her face. She'd swallowed water, and sputtered, choking, tearing at the surface of the lake. "Shit," he said, "hold on. I'm coming!"

She went under again and did not come up. Blood spread across the surface of the water, and John turned, kicking hard for the dock. Once there, he scrambled onto the rough, sun-warmed dock, grabbed up his clothes, and looked across the lake. Carla came back up, lifted out of the water by something under the surface. It was a fair distance across the water, and the sun dancing on the surface blinded John, but when he shielded his eyes with his hand, he saw the blade of a hatchet protruding from between Carla's breasts. Hatchetface carried her body in this manner, swimming toward the dock. John ran.

"He's here!" John said in a frenzied tone, racing toward the fire pit.

"Where's Carla?" Lisa asked.

"Dead!"

"Dead?" Tina asked.

"Yes!" John said, holding his clothes. "He's in the lake!"

Tina and Lisa looked to see Hatchetface standing on the dock, dripping water. He held Carla's body by her ankles with one hand, pulled his hatchet out of her with his free hand, then dropped her face-first onto the dock.

Still wet form the lake, John pulled on his clothes, and they clung to him. "Hide!" he whispered.

"Cabin 1?" Tina asked.

"It's splattered with blood, but we could go into Cabin 2," Lisa responded.

"Lisa," John said, "hand me my ammo box from the bench. Tina, get the bat out of the back. I'll get my bow and bolts.

*   *   *

Inside Cabin 2, they stood with their backs against the wall, just beside the front door. Tina gripped the softball bat, but her hands trembled. They'd brought in the lantern from the front porch and set it beside the bed.

"Shit," John said. "I forgot the gas. We'll need that, the kerosene, and the lanterns off the other porch."

"You can't go back out there," Tina hissed. "He'll kill you."

"I'll be back," John whispered. "I promise. Just stay away from the windows." He eased open the door and took off toward the truck.

The bow-gun lay across the foot of the bed. "Do you know how to use that?" Tina asked, pointing at it.

"Somewhat, my dad hunts with one."

Lisa loaded the bow gun and leaned against the wall, and the two girls stood on either side of the door. After a few minutes, a gunshot ripped through the silence, and John ran up onto the porch.

"Let me in!" he said. "It's just me."

John stepped inside, carrying two lanterns and the jugs. "What was that shot?" Tina asked, shutting the door and locking it.

"I shot him in the chest. Knocked him down for a minute, but he'll be back."

"He fell?" Lisa asked.

"No, shit. I shot him with a fucking .357."

"The officers shot him to pieces, and it didn't faze him."

Tina nodded. "Then he's playing with us," she said. "Wants us to think he's hurt. We need to lure him back to his gravesite somehow."

"I see you girls are ready for action," John said, pointing to the bow gun and softball bat.

"Hell, yeah," said Lisa.

"All right, then," John said, slipping his pistol in the waistband of his jeans. "Tina, get the jugs and a box of matches. Lisa, you grab a lantern. I'll take a lantern, too."

John went out of the cabin first, followed by Tina, then Lisa, who held the bow gun level, sweeping it form right to left. John stopped them at the fire pit, and they watched as smoke boiled out of the pots, smelling the burnt food. A dark cloud formed overhead, and the air cooled from an impending rain.

"We'd better move quick, before the rain starts in again," John whispered. "Whatever you do, don't run into the woods. Stay out in the open. He'll try to split us up and pick us off one at a time. He knows these woods better than we do."

The girls agreed. The three followed the trail lined with stones until they reached the cemetery. At John Lewis, Jr.'s grave, John poured gasoline through the broken slab, soaking the casket inside. When he was done, he set the jug on the ground.

"Lisa," he said, "you stand at the foot of the grave with the bow gun. I'll have my pistol. Tina, you have the gas and matches, so catch him on fire and show him that hell is where he belongs."

"Sounds like a plan to me," Tina said. She handed the bat to John. "Take this. I'll need a free hand. Let's get in place. You ready, Lisa?"

Clutching the bow gun, Lisa blew a lock of her hair out of her face. She nodded, then she and Tina hid themselves just inside the trees surrounding the cemetery. John sat with his back to the angle statue. "Hatchetface!" he yelled. "Come get me, you son of a bitch! I'm the one who murdered you! now Come and get your revenge!"

Hatchetface appeared at the outhouse and stopped. He looked at the cemetery and saw no one.

"Come on you, son of a bitch!" John said again.

Hatchetface started walking towards the cemetery. John gripped the bat in his left hand, and cocked the .357 with his right, now fully loaded. Hatchetface entered the cemetery and came to a stop beside his tomb. John rushed out from behind the statue and cracked Hatchetface in the head, and he fell over onto the broken concrete slab. Tina ran up to the grave, poured gasoline on him, then backed away, pouring out a trail of gas on the ground. She lit the gas with a match and it traveled to the tomb, catching Hatchetface on fire. John dropped the bat to the ground, pulled his .357 and shot Hatchetface in the back of the head as he tried to raise himself. The force of the shot threw Hatchetface forward, and he clawed at the broken concrete slab as he fell into the opening and down into the casket.

Crouched in the tree line with the bow gun, Lisa aimed at Hatchetface as black smoke rolled from his burning body. A light drizzle of rain started, threatening to put out the fire, and she rushed down to the tomb as John and Tina gathered behind the angle statue, pushing hard against it. Joining them, Lisa threw down the bow gun and threw her weight into the statue. The air hung heavy with the smell of burning flesh. The headstone shuddered, moving forward. "Keep pushing!" John yelled. But as he looked around the statue, he saw a flaming hand grip the broken edge of the grave's slab. "Push!" he yelled, and ran to the side of the grave, pistol drawn. He steadied himself, ready to fire, when a flaming hatchet spun end over end out of the grave, coming to rest in John's sternum. The blow picked him up off of his feet and sent him flying across a nearby grave. Hatchetface scrambled to claw his way out, but Tina and Lisa kept

pushing until the statue finally gave way. It fell forward,
driving its praying hands deep into the opening, crushing
Hatchetface and the casket.

The girls stood beside the grave for a few moments
until they were satisfied that the ordeal was over. "John,"
Tina whispered. She knelt beside him, his eyes still open
gazing at the sky. All she could do was nod her head in
disbelief. She looked over her shoulder. "Is that bastard
finally dead?" she asked Lisa.

"If that didn't do it," Lisa said, looking down into the
ruined tomb, "then nothing will stop him."

Tina shut her eyes and placed her hand on John's
face, closing his eyes with her fingertips. "That

motherfucker got his revenge," she said. "So it has to be over."

"What now?"

"We'll get an investigator out here to sort through all of this chaos," Tina said. "Then they'll have to believe us."

"I'm sorry, Tina," Lisa said.

"It's okay. He was an asshole, but I never stopped loving him, despite everything. Just leave everything. We'll take John's truck."

CHAPTER ELEVEN

Tina drove, and Lisa sat in the passenger seat as they went down the dirt road. They rode in since for over an hour until Tina pulled into the driveway of Lisa's house.

"You want to get out for a minute Tina?" Lisa asked. "You know—just in case he followed us. My parent won't be home till Friday."

Tina turned off the truck's engine. "There's no way he lived through that," she said, then stopped herself when she saw the look on Lisa's face. "Sure," she said. "I'll walk you to the door."

She walked Lisa to the door, and noticed what looked like plastic pool chairs beyond the white fence that kept the backyard from view. "Your parent have a pool?"

"Yeah," she said. "But it's been a while since I used it. You kind of forget it's there after a while. But when I was a kid I swam in it every day after school."

"I always wanted one."

Tina helped Lisa check the house, backyard, the pool, and the pool house before heading to the front porch again.

"See?" Tina said. "No boogeyman here."

Lisa laughed weakly. "Yeah. I guess I'm just being paranoid." She hugged Tina.

"You're safe," Tina said. "I'm headed to meet with an investigator. They'll have to believe us when they go back there and see it for themselves. Hell, what happened at the sheriff's office should be enough evidence to back up our story."

"Maybe when you come back we can go for a swim."

"All right," Tina said. "Sounds like a plan!"

*   *   *

It was dark by the time Deputy Sean Wynn followed Tina out to the camp. Carla's body had been moved from the dock,   and so had John's from the side of the tomb. Tina presumed that Hatchetface was still pinned beneath the concrete angel, but she couldn't be sure without digging through the rubble.

"Who could have moved all those bodies?" Tina asked herself.

"Everything seems normal here, except for that broken headstone," Deputy Wynn said as they walked back to his patrol car. The beams from their flashlight bounced along in front of them.

"So you don't believe me?"

"I didn't say that. I might come back here in the daylight and have another look. If your story checks out, there's bound to be evidence everywhere."

"What about what happened at the sheriff's office?" Tina said, trying to control herself. "You know a normal man couldn't have done all that."

Deputy Wynn stopped. "The official word on that is it was the act of a terrorist."

"You're shitting me?"

"Excuse me?"

"I'm sorry, officer. But you know and I know that's not true. And why would terrorists target a sheriff's office in the middle of nowhere? Waycross Georgia doesn't exactly make the national news."

Deputy Wynn kept walking. "Like I said, I'll send somebody out here tomorrow to look around."

"I thought you said you'd come back here yourself?"

"I forgot I had something else I had to do. But we'll check into it. I promise."

The deputy nodded to her as he opened the door of his car. "Have a good night, miss."

"Yes, sir and thanks," Tina said. She clicked off her flashlight.

After the deputy had left, Tina sat in the driver's seat of John's truck. She slammed her palms on the steering wheel. "Dammit," she whispered. "They're going to cover it up. All of it. A bunch of country bumpkin good old boys are going to throw it all away. And for what? Because it makes them look bad? Why not call the GBI? Or the FBI? It's not like nobody's going to wonder where all those people went. Jesus Christ." She reached to start the engine, but before she could something landed on the roof of the truck. She looked up just as the blade of a hatchet punched through the roof and buried itself in her skull.

*　　*　　*　　*

Lisa had tried to get some rest but couldn't. Every time she closed her eyes, she saw another flash of the horrors she'd witnessed. She went upstairs to her room and put on her neon green bikini.

She turned on the lights around the pool and went outside. The concrete around the pool was still warm the heat of the day, and she tried to keep her weigh ton her heels until she climbed onto the diving board. She thought back to all the times she'd done this as a child, how free and innocent she'd been, and how the water had always eased all of her worry after only a few minutes. But as she stood with her toes hanging off the end of the diving board, she pictured Hatchetface sitting on the bottom of the pool, waiting for her. She shook her and rubbed her eyes, then looked again. The bright lights recessed into the sides and bottom of the pool gave her a clear view—nothing was there.

"Calm down," she told herself aloud. "Tina's right. There's no way he survived that. He's dead. They're going to investigate, and everything's going to be all right."

She took a few steps back, then rushed forward and dove off of the diving board.

But before she hit the water, something happened.

She couldn't breathe, and it felt as though someone had kicked her in the back. The water was still warm, and the chlorine stung her eyes, but all she could see was red. She pushed for the surface, but she still couldn't breathe. Something heavy had lodged itself in her back, heavy enough to pull her down to the bottom. She kicked, fighting to reach the surface, but the weight pulled her further down. She felt cold, and her eyesight grew dim. Suddenly she no longer had the strength to fight. As she sank to the bottom, she looked up and saw someone standing on the diving board. He was impossibly tall, and she told herself this was all a bad dream, and she would wake up soon.

ERNEST ROBERSON SR-

BOOK TWO

THE ULTIMATE SLASHER

NINE MONTHS LATER

ERNEST ROBERSON SR-

CHAPTER ONE

"Four?"

"Four- Thirty," Lori said, ending the call.

"Who was that?" Her twin sister Torri asked, sitting on the bed.

Both girls along with six more were going to go camping at Camp Okefenokee for Spring Break in Waycross.

"That was Brandon, if you must know."

"The Mr. Georgia quarterback?" Torri asked.

"Yes, and he asked if we were ready. He said that they'd be here around four or four-thirty to pick us up."

Torri looked at her wristwatch on her left wrist.

"That's only fifteen, or forty-five minutes from now. Who's supposed to be going besides us?"

"Well, you know Brandon, his cousin Tyler Peters, Julie and Laura Bush, and Shawn and Dean Story," Lori said grabbing up her luggage from the bed.

Torri got off of the bed, grabbed her luggage as well, and followed Lori down the staircase. The two sat on the couch, waiting patiently until a knock on the front door startled them. Torri got up, unlocked the deadbolt, and twisted the gold doorknob. The door opened to reveal Brandon standing under the covered porch.

"You pretty girls ready?" he said with a grin

"Sure we are," Torri said.

*   *   *

Lori and Torri put their luggage into the green Town and Country van, then climbed in. Brandon got in the driver seat and they pulled out of the driveway. They were headed for Camp Okefenokee, sixty miles away. It was early April, and the sun would set in a just a few hours.   "It's supposed to rain this weekend," Brandon said, "so it might get nasty."

"Thank goodness we're staying a week then," Julie said, in the passenger seat.

"Don't worry," Tyler said from the back. "We got plenty of beer and liquor to last the whole week."

"Did you bring food?" Torri asked.

"No, we're going to eat you," Brandon said,

laughing as he drove.

"Sounds like a plan," Shawn said under his breath.

"You're both fucking perverts," Torri said.

"We left at four right?" Laura asked.

"Yes," Lori answered.

"Why?" Tyler asked.

"Because we should be nearing Highway 177."

Brandon continued driving on US 1 South when Laura

pointed.

"There, to your right. My phone says Dixon Memorial State Forest is in five miles."

"You girls have never been out this way, have you?" Brandon asked.

"Not really," said Torri.

"I have," Lori piped up. "When I was little."

"Shit," said Shawn. "That means none of us have been out here."

"Should be a good adventure, though," said Torri. "Right?"

Brandon drove on for until he spotted the dirt road to the right. He pulled the van off of the highway and onto the dirt road. It was now six o'clock and thunder rolled with echoes in the southern sky as lightning flashed and the wind gusted.

*　　*　　*

The eight sat in the van looking at the four cabins, talking while they waited for the rain to slacken. After making their sleeping arrangements, the conversation drifted to the legend of Hatchetface.

"Do you all believe that?" Brandon asked from the driver's seat, watching the rain pelt the windshield.

"Hatchetface?" Tyler scoffed. "If that shit was even half-real you'd have seen it in the papers or on the news. It's just a old story somebody cooked up to keep kids from hanging out around here and drinking and fucking."

Lori covered her mouth and tried to keep herself from laughing.

"His mama's supposed to live around here, you know," said Julie. "So why don't you go tell that to her face?"

"All right," said Tyler. "You're on. In the morning, we'll all go. And what do I get for such bravery?"

Julie smiled.

*   *   *   *

The rain eased up, and the eight got out of the van and unloaded their belongings. Lori and Tori unpacked their clothes and hung them up in the closet. All of the boys pushed their suitcases under the beds, preferring to leave their closets vacant. By seven o'clock the rain had stopped completely, though lightning streaked the sky to the south, reflected in the surface of the lake.

Once they'd unloaded everything, they sat around the fire pit on the wooden benches but couldn't build a fire since the wood was wet. Dean and Shawn had brought some old flashlights for everyone, and they used those against the falling darkness, passing a bottle of bottom shelf whiskey Brandon had taken from his father's liquor cabinet. By nine o'clock they all decided to call it a night and returned to their cabins.

Brandon woke up sweating. His stomach ached, and he held pressure on his abdomen with both hands. He got up, found the flashlight, and went out of the front door of Cabin 4. Outlined rock trails led him to the camp's out-house behind Cabin 1. He shined the flashlight in it, and then he went in and locked the door.

"Where's my medicine?" he asked himself, trying to remember where he put it when he packed his luggage.

He sat there for a long time, but his stomach only cramped while the flashlight stood upright, beaming its light on the outhouse ceiling. As he began to get up off of the toilet seat two arms reached out of the outhouse toilet grabbing him by the waist as he bent over to pull his pants up. Brandon struggled to break free, but the arms just pulled him down in between the toilet seat. Brandon's back broke and his face touched his pants at his shins. The flashlight now lay flat on the outhouse floor as he was pulled underneath into the hole.

*   *   *

Tyler was up at six. He was five-eleven, one hundred seventy pounds, with brown hair and brown eyes. He put on a pair of jeans, a plain white tee shirt, then slipped on his brown leather boots and tied them as he sat on the bed. He stood up, looked at the bunk beds and saw that Brandon had already left the cabin. He searched the fire pit, but saw no one. The sun was beginning to rise behind the cabins. In the weak morning light, he made his way to the van. The windows had been broken out, and someone had slashed each of the tires. As Tyler looked at the vandalized van he ran his hand through hair and exhaled deeply. "Fuck you, too, Brandon," he said quietly, and shrugged. Unfazed, he opened the side door and drug out several coolers and carried them to the fire pit, along with a small, portable grill. And a bag of charcoal.

Torri and Lori were the first the stumble out of their cabins. Still half-asleep, they'd been lured by the smell of the food. Both of them were blonde, standing a little under five feet tall and just at one hundred pounds. Their blonde hair fell to their shoulders and their blue-green eyes could stop men in their tracks. Both of them had been compared to models and centerfolds for so long that they just rolled their eyes and brushed off such comments. They were identical twins, and loved to play this up by dressing just alike. Today they'd coordinated white sleeveless tank tops and denim shorts with just enough inseam so as not to be arrested.

Julie was one hundred twenty pounds, blonde hair, with green eyes. She got up and looked out of the front door of her cabin. After she closed the door back she walked over to the closet and opened it. Julie put on a pair of jeans--pre-ripped at the knees—a brown tank top, and her white tennis shoes. When she was dressed she opened the door and went outside to where Tyler, Lori, and Torri were standing at the fire pit. It was nearing seven when Dean and Shawn got up. Shawn had sandy blonde hair, weighted one hundred eighty pounds, and had light green eyes. He dressed in khaki shorts with a light blue polo shirt and brown sandals. Dean was a hundred sixty with brown hair and eyes.

He dressed in jeans and a blue polo shirt and slip on brown

leather boots. Laura was the last one up. She had dark

brown hair and eyes weighed about hundred thirty pounds.

She got dressed in denim shorts, and a sleeveless sweater

top, a pair of brown   suede clogs. By seven thirty everyone

was standing around the fire pit, asking about Brandon.

"I don't know where he is," said Tyler, "but had

anybody had a look at the van?"

"No." Everyone replied.

They all walked from the fire pit to see it.

"That motherfucker!" Dean shouted. "That's my

mom's van! She's gonna kill me!"

"What the hell?" Torri said. "Why would he do that? Now we're all stuck."

"He's still pissed at me because I stole his girlfriend last year," said Dean. "I knew he was acting too buddy-buddy with me. Now it all makes sense. He's just been waiting to get me back."

"What if it wasn't Brandon?" asked Torri.

"Listen, people," said Sean, "before we start assuming it may not be what we're thinking."

"It wouldn't make sense for him to do this," Torri replied. "And hell yes I'm overreacting. You want me to stand here and look at this, knowing Brandon's missing, and not overact? You're fucking kidding me."

"I get it," Sean said, trying to keep calm. "It's bad. But before we jump to conclusions, let's see if we can get some help."

"It'll take forever for anybody to get out here," said Lori. "Besides, it's first thing in the morning in a weekend. Everybody I know is still in bed."

"No shit," Tyler said. "Tell me something that could actually help us."

"Well, if you'd shut up for one second, I would. If Brandon didn't do this, what if he walked over to the old Lewis place after he found this?"

"Good point," said Dean. "Except we don't know where it is. Let's just call the cops."

"Fuck that," Tyler chimed in. "With all this booze and not one of us is legal? I'm voting for going to the creepy house before I call my mom. She'll kick my ass right here in front of God and everybody. Hell, she'll probably put the hurt on all of us."

"Yeah," said Shawn, "my dad would freak the fuck out. I'm supposed to be at my cousin's house all week in Florida."

"Okay listen up then," said Tyler there's seven of us as of now until we can find Brandon. So here's what I suggest. Julie, Lori, and me will see if we can find the Lewis house. Everybody says it's close by. The rest of you all stay put in case if he comes back. But first, let's eat. If I know Brandon, it won't take long for some free food to bring him right back here."

CHAPTER THREE

Brandon never showed.

After they'd finished eating, Laura, Julie, and Tyler walked out onto the muddy dirt road they'd used to get into the campgrounds. Jut when they were about to turn back, they spotted a driveway of sand and walked down it. They came upon a house at the end of the road that looked abandoned and walked onto the porch. Tyler opened the screened door and knocked on the wooden door. He then closed the screen door back easily. An elderly lady with graying hair stood at the opened front door, behind the screen door.

"May I help you all?" The elderly lady asked in an undertone voice.

"Yes, ma'am," said Tyler, tying his best to sound respectful. "We were camping around here, and one of our friends went missing. We thought he might have come here."

The elderly lady nodded, as if she had been waiting for them.

"Come in," she said. They entered a small living room with no light fixtures, no television, and simple, sparse furniture. It looked as though it had been taken out of a history textbook, frozen in the way people in that area had lived over a century ago. "What are your names?" she asked.

Tyler sat between the girls on the old couch. "I'm Tyler," he said, "and this is Julie and Laura. Our friends name is Brandon."

The elderly lady began to laugh as she slowly rocked in her rocking chair in the corner.

"What's so funny?" Tyler asked, leaning forward.

"Once you come here," the lady said, "you can never leave. These are his woods, and everything in them."

Julie shifted and looked toward the door. "What are you talking about?"

But Tyler sat facing the woman. He had not moved. "I know what she's talking about," he said. "It's Hatchetface. He's you're son, right?"

"Smart boy," said the lady.

"Yeah. Smart enough to know that's an old story to scare kids. You're not fooling me lady. I'm sorry if you're lonely and you get a kick out of scaring teenagers that wander to your place, but I'm serious. We're looking for out friend. We've been respectful toward you, so we'd like it if you'd tell us if you've seen Brandon."

The elderly lady stopped rocking. "You're right, son," she said. "You've been nothing but cordial since you got here. So I'll tell you straight—run. Get as far away from here as fast as you can, and you might still have a chance."

Julie stood up and walked over to the elderly lady.

"Let me tell you something woman," Julie said in a low, firm voice,   "our friend is missing, and all you want to do is play games." She grabbed up a lantern that burnt low beside the woman on an end table.

"Julie no!" Laura yelled.

"You'll burn in hell, and I'll see that you do," Julie said, drawing back the lantern and swinging it downward on the elderly woman's head.

The woman caught on fire and cried in agony. From the porch, Hatchetface looked on from the front window. He took one deep breath and quickly exhaled. Tyler and Laura bolted through the door, but Julie calmly turned from the woman and walked out of the front door to see Hatchetface. The blaze a few months ago had further scarred him, leaving the left side of his face disfigured. All of his visible skin had hypertrophic scars, making it look as if he was melting. The smell of burning flesh hung thick in the air.

Tyler and Laura had stopped just long enough to witness the hopeless situation about to unfold before them. Though they wanted to run, both of them froze in horror as the hulking figure of Hatchetface grabbed Julie by the throat threw her to the sand just beyond the bottom step of the porch as easily as if she had been a ragdoll. She scooped up a fistful of sand as Hatchetface strode down the steps one at a time. She sat up, threw the sand in his eyes, and sprang to her feet.

Tyler and Laura, still too far away to help, pointed toward a small barn behind the house. Julie saw them, then shouted, "Get out of here!" to them. She ran towards the barn just as Hatchetface finished wiping the sand from his eyes. He followed.

Seeing there was no way to help their friend, Tyler and Laura ran back the way they'd come.

Once inside the barn, Julie quickly found a place to hide. Hatchetface swung open the huge double doors at the front of the barn and stepped inside. Julie looked around as she hid and spotted a pitchfork. She got to her feet, grabbed it, and held it firmly. As Hatchetface neared her, Julie held the pitchfork upright and rammed it into his abdomen. Julie turned towards the back door of the barn and ran towards it as Hatchetface pulled the pitchfork from his abdomen. He threw it down on the ground and pulled out his hatchet from the metal ring on his leather belt. Julie ran behind the barn towards the sandy road in which her, Tyler, and Laura had come to the house, followed by Hatchetface. The fire at engulfed the old house and columns of heavy black smoke rose into the sky.

CHAPTER FOUR

Julie had made it most of the way down the muddy dirt road towards the camp when she finally looked behind her. Seeing no one, she quit running and got off the road, deciding to walk just inside the tree line the rest of the way.

She came across a creek and knelt, cupped her hands together, and drew water. When she was done drinking she wet her face with the last bit of water which she'd drawn in her hands. Julie then stood from the creek and looked around. "Nothing not a sound," she thought.

A hand grabbed her by the throat. With her mouth opened Hatchetface rammed the wooden handle of his hatchet into her throat. Julie's head was forced upwards by the hatchet as he still held her with his left hand by the throat. Hatchetface then pulled his hunting knife from its sleuth and slit her throat crossways, revealing the hatchet handle. He put away the hunting knife, then grabbed the hatchet handle in her throat and pulled downward. The force as he pulled downward cut her bottom lip, shattered her jawbone, and slit the back of her throat.

*   *   *   *

Tyler and Laura had made it back to the camp. They sat around the fire pit with the others, who had been listening with confusion as they relayed their story.

"You're   joking, right?" Shawn asked.

"Is that black smoke a joke?" Laura asked pointing.

"Fuck you guys," Tyler said. "We need to act like a rock and roll. If you don't believe us, then just wait around for that thing to come kill you."

"Wait here for a minute and let me go to my cabin first though," Dean said.

"For what?" Tyler replied.

Dean ran and joined the others still sitting around the fire pit.

"What's so damn important we need to sit here and wait while that motherfucker's out there?" Tyler asked looking at Dean.

Dean reached behind him and pulled a .357 magnum out of his waistband. "This right here," he said, "will drop whatever comes through those woods."

"All right, okay just be careful with that thing," Shawn said.

"Okay then, there's three boys and three girls, let's pair up boy, girl," Tyler suggested.

"Lori and Shawn, Torri and Dean, Laura and I. So no matter what, stay by your partner because it's easier to pick off one at a time rather than two. And if we make it until night, assigned partners will share cabins together," Tyler said.

"So what do we need to do until then?" Shawn asked.

"We need firewood," Dean said.

"I still say that we should be finding a way out of here," Laura said.

"I agree with Laura," Lori said.

Torri nodded, but looked at her phone. "I'd call the cops, but my battery's dead. Anybody have any juice?"

"No," said Shawn. "We already tried that. The van's fucked so we can't charge our phones in there, and these cabins don't have any power, either."

"So it's settled," said Tyler. "We stand and fight. Anybody who wants to try and make it out of here alive by themselves is welcome to go."

No one moved to leave.

*   *   *

The six ate canned food from the coolers, choosing not to start a fire that might draw attention. No one had seen

Brandon, and some of them were skeptical about Julie's death. The tension in the group eased, and all but Tyler and Laura assumed it was all a prank, though they didn't say as much. As they finished eating, Torri, Lori, and Laura went to the lake and went swimming. While the three boys' kelp an eye on the camp and the three girls. In the south, a thunderhead was forming and was moving northward. Tyler and Shawn started drinking after they cleaned up after eating about one o'clock. The girls got out of the lake onto the wooden dock after hearing thunder and seeing lightning. They walked from the lake to the fire pit and started sipping on beer.

"You know I wonder if there are any more campers out here besides us," Laura asked.

"I really couldn't tell you," Tyler replied.

"It's beginning to get boring as hell," Lori said.

"Yes, I know. We have already lost two people, and everyone thinks that there's a grotesque killer on the loose in the woods. What kind of shit is that? Hell, we're all adults here, not children." Torri said.

"Hell, I wished that if there was a killer out here that he'd come and take me away from this fucked up spring break," Laura said.

"If I were you I'd watch what you wish for," Dean said.

The thunderhead was moving in quickly as the wind blew harder. The thunder and lightning were also getting closer as the six sat on the wooden benches, drinking at the fire pit.

"It's only a little after three," Torri said looking at her wristwatch.

Rain had begun to fall lightly. Thunder and lightning were right above the camp now and it looked as if it would settle in for the night. The couples went and occupied cabins one through three, neglecting cabin four. In cabin one Lori asked Shawn if he could cover his eyes while she changed her clothes. He agreed and respected her command. As she was in her unworn matching purple bra and panties Shawn stole a quick glimpse of her petite body. She put on a tank top and a pair of sweatpants. In Cabin 2 Torri didn't ask Dean to close his eyes as she stripped down to her pink bra and panties. She put on a tank top and shorts that were actually cut-off sweatpants. In Cabin 3 Laura got in the closet and changed, leaving the door cracked so she could see. Everyone was lying on their own bunk as the storm raged above them.

"You know," Laura said. "I'm wondering if Brandon and Julie are playing a joke on us."

"I don't know," said Tyler. "She's your sister. You should know her better than anyone."

"Well since you said it that way, what about your cousin then?" Laura replied.

"I guess you do have a point there. I honestly think we should go and look for them though," Tyler said.

"In this kind of weather?"

"Yes, why not? Do you have a raincoat, Laura? Because if I was missing I'd want you all to look for me. That would at least let me know that you cared."

"No, Tyler. I don't."

"Let's gather up the rest of the people," Tyler said, sitting up on the bottom bunk.

"You owe me one," Laura said.

"All right," Tyler said, smiling at her standing by the closet door. "You go on to Cabin 2 and I'll go get Lori and Shawn."

About five minutes later the six gathered in Cabin 2. The thunder and lightning still raged.

"All right," Tyler insisted, "here it is five o'clock. We still haven't heard from Brandon or Julie. So Laura, Torri, Dean, and I will go out to look for them. Shawn and Lori, you two stay here in case they come back."

The four left out of the cabin's front door.

ERNEST ROBERSON SR-

CHAPTER FIVE

"Lori," Shawn said as she lay on the bottom bunk.

"What Shawn?" Lori answered, opening her eyes to see him looking out the open front door.

"You're cute. Do you find me attractive?"

"Jesus, Shawn. Just come out and say it."

"Say what?"

"Say you want to have sex."

"Yeah. That."

"Why didn't you just say it then?"

"Because I'm kind of shy."

Lori got off of the bottom bunk and pulled off her clothes until she stood in her matching bra and panties.

"Well, you getting down here with me or not?" she said, getting back on the bottom bunk.

Shawn closed the cabin door, then unbuttoned his jeans and took off his shirt and threw it on top of Lori's clothes on the floor.

The two started off by kissing, but as soon as they'd taken off their underwear, the cabin door exploded in a hail of splinters.

"What in the hell! Get off of me Shawn," Lori said hysterically pushing him upward.

Shawn's foot got tangled up in the bedsheet and he tripped face first onto the floor. Lori got up and saw Hatchetface towering over them.

"What do you want from us?" Lori yelled out.

Hatchetface did not answer. He grabbed his hunting knife from his sleuth and cut Shawn from cut open his stomach with one swift slice. Lori had time to run past them and out of the doorway. She ran screaming for help, with Hatchetface close behind. As Hatchetface got close to her, he picked up the top of a can Shawn had earlier opened with his pocket knife. Lori tripped over an empty bottle of beer and fell into the fire-pit. She flipped over onto her back, but Hatchetface was already on top of her. He pinned her and, using the sharp edges of the can lid, sliced the corners of her mouth wide open before slashing her throat with the lid.

*   *   *

"Julie! Brandon!" Laura called out.

"If they're playing with us I'm going to kill them myself," Tyler said.

"This has been a messed up trip from the beginning."

"Tell me about it."

"What is that?" Laura asked as she stopped walking and pointed.

"Looks like an old cemetery," Tyler responded.

Tyler led the way as Laura followed him into the cemetery.

"This grave," said Laura, "it looks like it was busted open from the inside."

"We need to get back to camp before darkness catches us out here. Hopefully, Brandon and Julie are there when we get back."

Laura and Tyler walked back the way in which they'd walked. She stopped in her tracks when she saw Hatchetface.

"Do you see that Tyler?" Laura asked softly.

"Yeah," Tyler said whispering. "That's the same thing that was at the Lewis house. Head back to the camp. I'm going follow him."

Laura started walking away on the trail then Tyler stopped her.

"Here," said Tyler, "come take this flashlight and be careful going into camp because you know that Dean has that .357 magnum and he might be trigger happy."

"All right," Laura said, walking away on the trail, gripping the flashlight with both hands.

*   *   *   *

Laura came into camp by the outhouse and walked past Cabin 1. As she stood in the middle of the camp site at the fire-pit, she noticed the faint light of a kerosene lantern inside Cabin 2. Laura walked up the four steps and saw what was left of the door. Dean and Torri were sitting on the bottom bunk, looking at the pool of blood on the wooden floor.

"What's happened?" Laura asked.

"This isn't a joke," Dean said. "This is real red blood. And I don't think it's from an animal."

"Where's Tyler?" Torri asked.

"We saw what looked like a person in the woods. We thought it was the same guy that we saw at the old Lewis house, and Tyler decided to follow him."

"Follow him?" Torri said. "Why? So he can get murdered?"

"I say we go and find him now, and get the hell out of here," said Dean. "If not, we're all going to die here."

Dean and Torri got up from the bottom bunk and the three walked down the four steps. Laura led with her flashlight in her hand. Dean brandished the .357 magnum in his right hand, and Torri followed with a flashlight. The three went between cabins 1 and 2, then into the woods. The three had walked about fifty yards into the woods behind the cabins when they met Tyler.

"You all right?" Laura asked.

"Yes, I got stuck in this damn slew."

Tyler stood upright and leaned on a large cypress tree to his left. Lightning revealed the large man standing by the cypress tree with a military trench shovel leveled with Tyler's head.

"Watch out!" Dean yelled from behind them as thunder sounded.

"What?" Tyler asked.

Hatchetface rammed the shovel into Tyler's right cheek bone and quickly lifted upward towards the tree. The shovel stuck into the large cypress.

"The son of a bitch is real!" Dean screamed.

Hatchetface walked through the wet, boggy slew with ease. Dean leveled the .357 magnum up at Hatchetface as the thunder, lightning, and rain all raged above him.

"You two," Dean yelled to Torri and Laura, "shine your flashlights on him!"

Dean fired and hit his mark directly between Hatchetface's eyes. Hatchetface fell backward onto a pointed tree stump. The stump impaled him, and he lay motionless.

"Oh my God," Laura said. She turned her flashlight away, unable to look at the gruesome scene any longer.

The three then turned around and walked back into the campsite.

CHAPTER SIX

With the three in cabin one, Torri and Laura sat on the

bottom bunk and Dean faced them, chattering like a

madman.

"Listen," he said, "I don't know why that

motherfucker out there wants us dead, but he does. And I

know this for sure, there use to be eight of us as now we're

only three strong. I don't know if there's a good plan, or

idea that'll work for us. But we can't split up, and we can't

just sit here like sitting ducks and get picked off. It's like a chess game. We've lost a lot of our valuable pieces and we're just out here flying blind."

"Well, what do you insist on us doing?" Laura asked.

"There have to be other people living or camping around here," Torri said.

"All right. We'll try that then," Dean said, opening the cabin's front door.

The three had gone out of cabin with Laura leading the way with her flashlight. They walked by the van, then down the overgrown alley. The weather still wasn't cooperating as the rain fell steady and hard, the thunder boomed above, and the lightning lit up the night sky.

"Whatever we do let's make sure that we stay on the road," Dean said, bringing up the rear.

As they walked from the overgrown alley rocks underneath their feet made a crunching sound, but they kept going.

*   *   *

"Hey, you two," Laura said excitedly, "I see the highway up ahead."

"Can we please rest for a minute? My legs are feeling rubbery," Torri said as they reached the blacktop road.

"Yes, I've got to pee," Laura said.

"Hell, I've been too afraid to stop and piss when I had to go, I just piss myself," Dean said.

"And I thought that I was the only one that was doing that," Torri said as they stood in the middle of the highway.

"If I were you I wouldn't go too far into those woods," Dean said.

Laura peed stood back up, pulled up her panties and pants, and then leaned over to pick up her flashlight. She put the flashlight in her back right pocket of her pants and began walking back towards Dean and Torri standing on the highway. Laura was quickly swept off of her feet. Two nylon ropes had each ankle making her look as if she was a Y hanging in the air about five feet off of the ground. She could touch the ground with her hands. As Dean and Torri still stood waiting for her on the shoulder of the paved road, Hatchetface his hatchet. With one swipe, the sharp hatchet cut her in half. The pieces of her body hung from the trees by the nylon ropes. Hatchetface stood looking at the corpse, then took a deep breath in and let it out in a slow, measured breath. He looked at Dean and Torri on the shoulder of the road.

Dean told Torri to shine her flashlight towards Hatchetface. When she had the flashlight held steady on him Dean fired twice hitting Hatchetface in the heart and stomach. Once again he fell to the ground and Dean lowered gun. He grabbed Torri by the hand and they sprinted off into the night until they had to stop.

"Well," Dean said, gasping for breath, "it's only you and me now."

As the two walked Northeast, Hatchetface stood watching

from behind them in the middle of Highway 177..

CHAPTER SEVEN

"You know I really believe that if we were to live through this night until morning that we'd survive," Torri said.

"I agree with you somewhat," Dean replied, looking at her.

The rain had ceased to a drizzle, but the thunder raged on around them, and as the two looked ahead of them a flash of lightning revealed to them Hatchetface standing in the road.

"Oh shit, not again," Dean said as the two stopped in the road.

Torri held the flashlight on Hatchetface once again and Dean fired twice hitting him in the right shoulder and chest, but he didn't fall.

"Shoot again!" Torri yelled holding the flashlight.

"I'm out of bullets! Run into the woods and hide. Maybe the morning light will find you alive and spare your life."

"I won't leave you, Dean."

"Please just go," Dean begged. "Don't let him kill us both."

Torri ran off into the densely wooded swamp land. Dean swung, hitting Hatchetface repeatedly in the face, and even used the empty gun to pistol whip him. But Hatchetface was never fazed nor moved an inch. He let Dean continue for a while, as if to amuse, himself, then punched Dean in his chest with enough force to penetrate the boy's ribcage. Hatchetface then used his other hand to pull apart Dean's chest.

*　　*　　*

Dawn broke.

The rain had ceased, although a few clouds remained in the overcast sky. Torri was now moving again and crossed back over Highway 177 thinking she'd found US-1. Little did she know that she was heading back towards the campsite.

As she came out of the thick swamp land, she stumbled back onto the dirt road. I her exhaustion and terror, she didn't realize her error until she passed the destroyed van and found herself trapped once more among the four cabins. She dropped to her knees and cried, overcome with disbelief and fear. She heard something behind her, and turned to see Hatchetface standing beside the van. She ran towards the lake and slipped into the water without a sound, watching the shore for any sign of movement as she eased underneath he dock. Torri watched him as he walked slowly along the shore, then passed by. Still, she waited long after he was out of sight, before she headed back to the van. Once there, she pulled on the hood release button through the shattered window. She found a plastic drink bottle and laid it on the ground before opening the hood. Torri took the caps off of the battery and poured the battery acid from it into the bottle with ease. When the bottle was half full she figured that she had enough to do the job. She put the bottle down again, holding the battery against the van with her left hand. Torri then eased the battery down with both of her hands, trying to be as quiet as she could. After she placed the battery back in its place, she took off her shirt and pants because the acid had splashed onto her without her noticing. She wiped herself off, then picked up the bottle and twisted the top onto it. She went down the trail beside Cabin 1 in her matching panties, bra, and tennis shoes.

*   *   *

Torri saw Hatchetface standing beside the empty tomb at the back of the cemetery. At first she froze, holding the bottle of battery acid in the crook of her arm. But as she watched him, she saw no sign of movement. It seemed he hadn't noticed her. Then she devised her plan—she would sneak up on him. As quietly as she could, she took great pains to control her movements as she crept around the perimeter of the cemetery, making sure to stay within the tree line where she wouldn't be visible. As she made her way around the cemetery, she kept a close eye on Hatchetface, noting that he had not moved. As she neared him, she twisted the top off of the bottle of battery acid. She stepped out from the protection of the tree line and took a few tentative steps toward him, then something happened. Some rush of courage unknown to her before that moment welled up from within her and she ran, focused on the towering menace

before her.

"Hey, you motherfucker!" Torri yelled.

In an instant, Hatchetface spun to face her and raised

his hatchet high. But before he could bring it down in its

unstoppable arc, Torri   splashed the acid into his eyes,

squeezing the bottle flat with all the strength her grip would

allow. The battery acid spewed from the bottle. Hatchetface

dropped the hatchet. He covered his face with both hands

and stumbled backward until his heel caught on a chunk of

the broken statue, and he fell into the open grave. Torri

gasped and stood still for a moment, waiting to see if he was

finally finished. But there was no movement form the grave.

She looked closer to see that the bit of statue had been the

tip of one of the angle's wings. Had she had time to think

about it, she might have smiled at the thought. But the only thing that drive her at that moment was fear. She knew he would come back, as he always had. She turned ran back up the trail. Too afraid to look back, she kept her eyes and her thoughts centered on what was in front of her. But as she passed the fire pit, something made her look over her shoulder.   Just as she'd thought, she saw Hatchetface lagging behind, lumbering forward as though he had all the time in the world.

CHAPTER EIGHT

Torri tripped. As she lay on her stomach, she turned her head to the side and spotted the end of a hollow log in a clearing just inside the woods. It was small, but if she curled up tight enough, she might fit. She pushed herself up into a sitting position, then half-crouched, half-ran through the tangled brush until she'd made it to the log. As she looked out of the end which she faced about a minute later she found herself looking at Hatchetface's pants and his muddy brown boots. Torri stayed as still as she could, taking small breaths of air until he finally turned and walked the way back the way he'd come. Then she thought about Lori's phone in the cabin.

*   *   *   *

She guessed that she'd been hiding in the hollowed out log for at least two hours.   She'd grown even more tired, and she was hungry. Her tongue stuck to the roof of her mouth from thirst. She crawled out of the log.

She walked back onto the gravel road, checking her surroundings constantly. Once she'd made it to the van, she eased her way to the passenger's side, blocking her from the view of anyone inside the camp.

She took a deep breath, but as she let it out, she almost sobbed. The sudden burst of fear overtook her, but she clamped her palm over her mouth until it passed. Before she had time to talk herself out of it, she ran on her tip toes until

she'd cleared the steps and into the splintered wreckage of

the door. She saw the puddle of blood, then opened the

closet and found Lori's bag. She pulled the bag out into the

middle of the floor and searched for her sister's phone until

she finally found it in a side pocket and laid the phone on

the edge of the bottom bunk bed.   As she looked for some

clothes in the small closet, she happened to turn around.

Hatchetface stood without a sound at the bottom of the steps.

The clothes in her arms fell to the floor, and she grabbed the

phone and slipped it in her bra. She looked around, grabbed

the empty suitcase, and used it to smash out the back

window of the cabin. Hatchetface was nearing the last step

as she put the suitcase on the bottom part of the broken

window. She stood on the bottom bunk as she held the

suitcase and climbed out of the window head-first. As she was about to jump down onto the ground outside Hatchetface grabbed her by her hair and started pulling her back up. But then she spotted a piece of broken glass, barely holding on in the sill of the window. She snatched it loose. Looking up, she saw Hatchetface had leaned out of the window to grab her, and he'd remained in this position—leaving his neck exposed.   She stabbed him with the glass and pushed it in as deep as she could. She fell onto her back but swung her arms out and lapped the ground the way she'd learned to do in tumbling class. It broke her fall just enough, and she got to her feet, grabbed the phone out of her bra, and ran.

*   *   *

Standing in the middle of Highway 177, Torri turned held the phone to her ear.

"Come on," she pleaded, "come on, dad. Pick up. Pick up! Please!"

Finally, she heard her father's voice on the other end of the line.

"Dad!" she screamed. "Thank God! I need you. Listen. Just listen. I don't have time to explain, but I need you and everybody you can get to come Camp Okefenokee. Bring guns and the police."

She paused for a moment, then responded.

"No, this phone's about to die. You have to call. The cops won't believe me, anyway. They'll think it's a prank. But they'll listen to you. And Dad? I love you." She took the phone away from her ear and looked at the blank screen. "Shit," she muttered.

Moments later, a truck rumbled toward her on the highway, and she jumped up and down, waving her arms.. The driver stopped and Torri walked up to the candy apple red truck.

"Hey, darling you need a ride?" The driver asked.

"If you don't mind, I need to get into town."

"Well my name is Troy Phillips, and yours?"

"Torri Vicks."

"The way that you're dressed I was thinking that we could go back to my place and I could give you a good time."

"Please, mister. I just need a ride."

"That's what I'll give you."

"Fuck you."

After Torri said that, Hatchetface now stood on Highway 177 looking at her. He pulled out his hunting knife from its sheath and walked in front of the candy apple red truck. He stopped in front of the truck and used the knife to scratch the paint from the driver's side to the passenger's side of the hood. Troy blew the truck's horn.

"You son of a bitch! What are you doing?"

Troy stomped the gas, but Hatchetface made no sound as the truck rolled over him. Troy put the truck in park, grabbed his shotgun from the passenger side of the truck, and get out. Torri, however, did not stay to see how the confrontation would end. Troy stood on the highway with the gun as the truck idled. Hatchetface sat up in the road and got to his feet. Troy shot him once, but it was as if Troy had thrown a pebble at the grotesque thing before him. The gun clicked and Troy swung it at Hatchetface, who held his right arm up. The gun shattered on impact. Stunned, Troy dropped the remains of his weapon onto the asphalt. Hatchetface grabbed Troy by the neck and quickly lifted him and slammed him down to the blacktop. Hatchetface placed his boot firmly between Troy's shoulder blades, then grasped him by the neck with his huge hands. In one quick pull, he removed Troy's spine and skull from his body. He threw it into the ditch and looked down the road.

CHAPTER NINE

Torri had found a clear embankment and laid on her back,

exhausted. As she looked up at the sky, the rain clouds

rolled in and she knew that it would rain again before the

day was over with. As she glanced into the sky a silver cab

Dodge Ram passed by. She jumped up and ran into the

middle of the road, waving her arms, but the truck had

already travelled too far for the driver to spot her. "Dad!"

she yelled, but her voice sounded small and weak. She knew

the chances of him looked back down the road were slim.

She knew Hatchetface would have moved the body, and

probably the truck. They were headed into a trap, and there was nothing she could do.

*   *   *

The Dodge Ram pulled up to the campsite. The driver, Vince Vicks, opened the door and got out. He was in his early forties and had brown hair and eyes. He scanned the campground, looking for his daughters Lori and Torri. Behind him, Bill Story opened the passenger door. The father of Shawn and Dean, he stood five nine, two hundred thirty pounds, with green eyes, and sandy blonde hair.   He took his place beside Vince, as the other fathers stepped out of the truck: Wayne Bush, who was Julie and Laura's dad, six- four, 250 lbs., with black hair, and brown eyes; Kenny Peters, the father of Tyler, weighed one twenty, with gray hair and blue eyes. Jack Peters was the last to step out of the truck. He weighed the same as Kenny and had gray hair, but his eyes were green.

The men looked at the van, the turned away and began calling out to their children. Vince walked back to the bed of his truck and retrieved a hunting rifle with a scope. Bill, Wayne, Jack, and Kenny followed, slinging their rifles over their shoulders by nylon straps. Jack, however, carried had a .357 revolver in the waistband of his jeans, and he adjusted it as walked away from the truck..

"I don't know what's going on here," said Vince, "but I sure as hell don't like it."

"You sure this isn't just some prank they're pulling on us?" Jack asked.

"Not a chance," Vince replied. "My daughter wouldn't joke like this. Whatever's going on, it's real."

They began their search at the fire pit.

*   *   *

Torri had almost neared the graveled road. And as she realized she couldn't just waltz up to the campsite with several armed grown men on the hunt for whoever took their children. Instead of following the gravel road into the campsite, she veered right off of the highway and cut into the woods in search of the hollow log she'd used to hide from Hatchetface.

Torri quietly made her way back to the hollow log. She squatted and looked around to see Julie and Laura's dad, Wayne Bush, not far away through the trees. For a moment, she thought of calling out to him, but then she remembered the unstoppable brutality of Hatchetface and crawled inside the log. She felt a little more secure now knowing that all of the kid's dads were here with guns, but she resolved to stay in hiding until the men had killed Hatchetface once and for all. Until they had, she knew there would be no escape for any of them.

ERNEST ROBERSON SR-

CHAPTER TEN

All three men gathered at the tomb in the cemetery. Vince laid his rifle on top of   the broken slab.

"What do you make of it?" Jack asked.

"I'm not for certain," Vince said, rubbing the slab with his hand.

"Does it have a name or date etched on it somewhere?" Bill asked.

"Nothing," Vince said.

Vince balanced himself and leaned forward to look into the tomb.

"You see anything?" Jack asked.

"Nope," Vince replied.

"What do you think happened? Graverobbers?"

"Could be," said Vince, "but look at the way the slab is broken. Unless somebody arranged to that way after it was smashed, it looks like somebody broke it from the inside."

"Hold up now," said Bill, "you're trying to tell me a fucking a ghost story right now? Where are our kids?"

"Ghost story?" Jack asked. "You mean that old shit about Hatchetman or whatever?"

"Hatchetface," said Vince. He took up his rifle. "I'm not saying anything yet. But I get the feeling some real bad shit went down here. If we're gonna find our kids, we'd better get a move on."

*   *   *

Torri looked down the length of the log, past her feet. Wayne hadn't moved—she assumed he was standing guard for the other men. He'd been there for a while, so it was no surprise to Torri when Wayne leaned his rifle against a nearby tree and took a seat on the ground. Before she realized what she was seeing, Hatcheface appeared, as though he was a part of the woods themselves. He covered

Wayne's mouth and drug him away into a thicket of bushes and crushed his jawbone with one hand. Hatchetface lifted his right boot up and stomped   Wayne's head, causing the man's brains to explode out of the top of his skull. His eyeballs rolled onto the ground. When Torri looked back out of the hollow log she saw that Wayne was now gone, he wasn't where he once sat. As she continued looking out of the hollow log she saw Hatchetface walking by where Wayne had sat. He stopped, then turned in Torri's direction. He took up Wayne's rifle where it rested, leaning against the tree, and kept walking.

*   *   *

Kenny was watching Vince, Bill, and Jack as he knelt on his right knee on top of the hill. Hatchetface held the rifle by the barrel with both of his hands and drew back, ramming the rifle's stock into Kenny's back. Kenny fell to the ground, limp and lifeless, and Hatchetface dropped the rifle. Jack looked towards the hill behind them.

"That's odd," Jack said.

"What?" Bill replied, turning towards the hill.

"Kenny and Wayne are gone."

"They might've hid in some bushes so they couldn't be seen," Vince said.

About that time, Vince's cell phone rang. Jack and Bill remained quiet before Vince answered his phone and remained so until he ended the call.

"Who was that?" Bill asked, looking at Vince.

"Jamie," Vince said.

"Oh, the wife," Jack said.

"She was just checking up on us, but I could hardly hear her. She was in and out and there was static. You know how these cell phones work out here in the middle of nowhere."

Torri noticed her dad had his cell phone's ring tone. She knew there wasn't much time before Hatchetface found them. She slid out of the log and cut through the woods, headed for the lake.

CHAPTER ELEVEN

Torri went to the end of the dock and started jumping up

and down. She called out Hatchetface's name and her voice

echoed over the lake and throughout the woods. Vince, Bill,

and Jack saw Torri in only her panties and bra on the dock

as they stood behind the vandalized van and Vince's truck.

She saw Hatchetface standing at behind one of the

cabin's blocked from the view of the men. She stopped

jumping and fell silent. Bill went into the woods to the right of where the three men stood in front of the cabins and towards the lake. Vince went towards the outhouse and circled behind the cabins. Jack stayed put, acting as the lookout. Bill found a clearing which would give him the opportunity for a great shot towards the dock. There was only a dead tree here, which he could lay on his belly and prop his gun on for a precise shot. Bill looked through his scope to see a huge, grotesque person in front of Torri with his back to him. Vince had taken the same approach as Bill by the bank of the lake. He found a fallen tree, laid on his belly, and rested his rifle on the fallen tree. Both Vince and Bill had Hatchetface in their crosshairs, ready to fire whenever Torri jumped into the water. Hatchetface now stood in front of her on the dock, holding his hatchet high above his head. Torri walked backward until she'd reached the end of the dock, then dove off, never losing sight of

Hatchetface as Bill and Vince fired.

*   *   *

Torri had swum underneath the dock under water, then

veered to her right and slowly popped her head up from the

water. She was now able to stand up in the water as she

turned and looked back towards the end of the dock to see a

motionless Hatchetface face down with one hand dangling

in the water. Bill and Vince walked slowly onto the wooden

dock.

"We nailed that bastard," Bill said, walking with

Vince towards the end of the dock.

Vince and Bill were giving high fives over the corpse as

Torri was walking out of the lake. She looked back at them

and knew that this was not the end of the nightmare. Now she felt that she was to blame for what might happen to her dad, Bill, and Jack. She made her way past the slew behind cabin 4 and went towards the tomb. Torri knew that she had to hide again but wanted to stay close just in case they tried leaving in the truck. So she went and hid once again in the hollow log.

*　*　*

Hatchetface laid motionless on the wooden dock. Vince and Bill turned towards Jack, who was standing by the passenger's side of the truck. Seeing no movement from the corpse, they walked away.

"Let's find Torri and get the hell out of here!" Vince said. "This shit is insane."

"Way ahead of you, brother," replied Bill. "Maybe she knows where the others are."

"Maybe so," Vince replied walking off of the dock with Bill.

Bill and Vince walked to the truck and met up with Jack.

"What now?" Jack asked. "Is anybody gonna call the cops?"

"Go ahead," said Bill. "You won't get any cell reception for another twenty miles. This whole area's a dead zone."

"We find our kids and go home," Vince said. "Once they're home safe, we'll go to the cops." He nodded to Bill, and said, "Take my truck and drive along the in both directions. If they're still alive, they'd stick to the major roadways. And if they're stuck out in these woods, me and Jack will find them."

As Vince and Jack walked away towards the cabins, Bill got into the truck, started the engine, and put the truck in reverse. He put the truck in drive and started down the overgrown alley. When he got to the gravel road he saw Hatchetface standing in the middle of the road. Bill pressed the brake and put the truck in reverse. The truck didn't move. Bill looked, stunned, as he realized that Hatchetface had squatted and gripped the truck under the front bumper, rendering the truck immobile. Bill dropped the shifter back into park, but it was already too late. With uncanny speed, Hatchetface slipped around to the driver's side of the truck, smashed out the glass in the driver door, and grabbed Bill by the neck. But instead of killing him right away, he spotted the rifle beside Bill's right leg and grabbed it with his free hand. Hatchetface slammed Bill's head into the windshield, smashing a hole in the windshield. He then put the gun through the hole, and then he pulled his head to the outside of the truck's driver side door window and bent the rifle's barrel around Bill's neck.

ERNEST ROBERSON SR-

CHAPTER TWELVE

Vince and Jack had separated, calling out the children's names. But no one answered.

Jack held his .357 revolver with both hands. Hatchetface walked up behind him and put his hand on top of Jack's head. As Jack screamed, Hatchetface put four of his fingers into Jack's mouth and then pulled downward, tearing his jaw from his face. Jack fell face forward into the slew.

Vince heard Jack's scream and managed to walk through the slew and mud towards where Jack should've been. It started to rain, but without any thunder or lightning. The wind gusted.

*   *   *

Torri peeked out of the hollow log and saw no one. She crawled out of the hollow log, stood up, and looked around wondering which way she should go. Torri decided to go right towards the graveled road. Once there she seen her dad's silver Dodge Ram parked at the end of the overgrown alley. She walked up to it and saw Bill Story with a rifle twisted around his neck, hanging out of the windshield. So she walked on into the camp site by the alley. Behind Cabin 1, she saw her dad Vince standing on the trail. Torri yelled out his name. As her dad turned around and faced her, Hatchetface walked out from between two of the cabins. Hatchetface turned towards Vince as he had his 7mm rifle pointed upward at him. Vince knew that he couldn't take a shot with Torri in the background, so he lowered then turned the 7mm rifle around and held it by the barrel, ready to swing it. As Hatchetface walked towards him he pulled his hatchet from the ring on the tool belt. Once Hatchetface was close enough to him Vince swung the rifle shattering the wooden butt of the 7mm against Hatchetface's body. Hatchetface then swung his hatchet level at Vince's head and beheaded him as Torri watched from the van. She turned and ran into the grown up alley way, and onto the gravel road.

*　　*　　*

Torri looked back on the gravel road to see Hatchetface on her heels, so she ran to her left off of the gravel road, into the woods. She hadn't run too far off of the road when she fell into some old, tangled barbwire left over from a fence that had rotted away years ago. The barbs on the wire stuck into the flesh of her legs and brought trickles of blood that mixed with the rain. Hatchetface caught up to her and looked down at Torri tangled in the barbwire on the ground.

"You don't have to hurt me! Please, Hatchetface!" Torri pleaded, looking up at him.

When she called his name he looked down at her. Hatchetface pulled out his hatchet again from the ring on his tool belt. He then picked Torri up and began wrapping barbwire down her arms as she begged. Hatchetface used his hatchet to cut the barbwire. He also tied the barbwire around seven-inch cypress trees that were about four feet apart from one another. When he was done, blood ran from her wrist and ankles. Torri looked like an X in the middle of the two cypress trees. Hatchetface then wrapped two more strands of barbwire over her forehead down to her breast, and in between her crotch. He tightened the strands of barbwire with his hands. Then he walked around Torri as she continued to beg one last time as he was inspecting his work. As he looked at the strands of barbwire that went over her body and between her midsection he could tell that she shaved there. The strands came on up in the center of her abdomen, between her breast, and in between the center her forehead. Then it went centered over her head, down her backbone, into her ass.

"Please, Hatchetface," she whimpered, "you can just let me go. I promise not to tell anyone about what happened out here. Just please let me go home to my friends and family. You've killed my dad and sister already."

The rain began falling harder as Hatchetface put his hatchet back into the ring on his tool belt. As the rain dripped off of her body he grabbed a hold of the barbwire in the center of her back with his right hand and snatched it as hard as he could. The force of the pull ripped Torri's body in half. Her right and left side hung by her wrist and ankles from the two cypress trees as Hatchetface dropped the strands of barbwire on the ground and walked away from the divided corpse.

BOOK THREE

REAWAKENED

ERNEST ROBERSON SR-

CHAPTER ONE

13 Months Later…

A silver Ford crew cab pulled into an empty parking space in front of Hank's Restaurant in Waycross, GA. The waitress working was twenty-three year old Abi Hines. She poured coffee for a couple as the two men got out of the truck and shut the doors. They were dressed in suits. They talked and grinned as they walked towards the glass entrance door of the restaurant. Inside, the smell of sausage and bacon filled the air as the two men sat in a booth in the far corner of the restaurant. As they talked, Abi walked towards them to take their orders.

"Morning," Abi said with a smile.

"Morning," they both replied back.

"What will you all be drinking this morning?"

"I'll take orange juice," one man said.

"Same here," the other said, looking up from the laminated menu.

Abi wrote on her order form. She suddenly stopped writing.

"Will this be together?" she asked.

"Yes," said the man who'd ordered his drink first.

"Are y'all ready to order, or do you need more time?"

"I think that we're ready," both men agreed.

"What will it be then?" Abi asked with her pen in her right hand.

"I'll take the original grits, eggs, and sausage," the man who ordered his drank said.

The other man looked at the menu. Then he ordered an omelet and hash browns with toast.

"Would you also like toast?" Abi asked the first man.

"Sure. With grape jelly."

Abi finished writing the order down on her pad.   "I'll be back with your drinks," she said, and walked towards the wooden counter. The two men sat talking to one another as customers began filling up the empty tables in Hank's. But the two men never paid any attention to the people coming and going around them as Abi carried them their food.

"Do you both need anything?" Abi asked, handing them their food.

"No, ma'am. I believe we're good for now."

As the two men finished their breakfast, an older gentleman pulled up a chair at the booth with them. The elderly man introduced himself as Maynard Phillips.

"So you guys or one of you is Hurley Edenfield, I take it."

Both men looked at each other, then towards Maynard.

"That'll be me, sir," Hurley said picking up his cup of orange juice. He took a drink and sat it back onto the tabletop. "Why do you ask?"

"It's not that I'm asking, but the well-dressed lawyers, bankers, and such don't eat here."

"So we're out of place here?" Hurley asked.

"Somewhat, but don't get me wrong. You're welcome here. So you're the guy that bought all of the land from Highway 177 back to that camp on both sides of that Lewis home?"

"I did, Mr. Maynard. I guess news travels fast around here. I assume that you also know that I'm building a ten room motel which is near completion."

"I do, but it's not what you're doing out there on the land. It's that many town remember the killings that took place there. Mr. Edenfield, many of the county's residents believe that the land is cursed by the deathless one, Hatchetface."

"Hatchetface?" Hurley asked, as he began laughing with his associate.

Hurley picked up his glass once again and drank from it.

"Mr. Maynard, did any of the timber crew or land development crew go missing?"

"No, sir," Maynard replied.

"But the residents believe Hatchetface still seeks revenge and damnation for anybody that goes there?" Hurley's associate asked.

"Yes. Yes, indeed. It's been twenty-two months since a group of five went out there and never came back.

Prior to that, those blamed for John Lewis Junior's death, there were six of them that just vanished," Maynard replied.

"Mr. Maynard," Hurley said, "you have a great imagination. Good for telling stories around a campfire."

"Hell, I think that dementia has finally set in," Hurley's associate replied, laughing.

"We're concerned for our safety, and for the safety of anybody who goes out there," Maynard said.

"But it's only March, Maynard. Summer is still a few months away, and the place isn't even ready." Hurley stood up. He reached into his pocket and pulled out a crisp twenty dollar bill and put it on the table for the tip. He looked at Maynard and told him to have a nice day. Hurley and the associate walked to the counter to pay the bill and left out of Hank's Restaurant.

"What a character," Hurley said getting into the silver Ford truck.

CHAPTER TWO

It was now 8:30. Hurley and his associate rode on US 1 South until they saw Highway 177 South.

"You know," Hurley said as he drove, "no one except for the development company has been around the Okefenokee Swamp grounds for…what did Maynard say…two years? The crews came in and built an entire motel, and no one has been killed or accounted for as a missing person."

He turned onto Lewis Road which, now pave in asphalt, and drove towards the once overgrown path leading back to the cabins. There was now a parking lot in front of the motel with white lines for vehicles to park. The timber crew thinned a lot of timber to open the view of the renovated area. The cemetery had been cleaned up and now had a four foot chain link fence around it behind the motel rooms. Electricity was now supplied, as was the water from a deep well. The motel even sported basketball court and a tennis court motel, with a mini golf course just beyond them. The trail to the lake had little pebbles and the dock had been redone with a diving board built onto it. All that was left was the painting the rooms and the outside of the motel's stucco walls. Hurley pulled into the parking lot, stopped, and turned off the truck's engine. The two men got out and set to the task of performing a thorough walkthrough of the facilities.

*   *   *

Three months passed, and the month of June saw Mr. Hurley Edenfield holding a big pair of scissors getting ready to cut the red ribbon for the Grand Opening of Southern Fanciful Resort. Mayor Jim Dodge was there, along with a few contractors and county politicians, ready for photo ops. They all stood together as Hurley cut the ribbon, and the photographer took the picture. Afterwards everyone talked, walked around looking at the motel outside and in the rooms. Between rooms 1-5 and 6-10 was an ice machine, stationed two vending machines for sodas and snacks. People walked down the pebble trail to the lake and walked onto the wooden dock. At noon everyone began leaving and when everyone was finally gone, Hurley and his associate, Mike Jones, stood talking in the center of Southern Fanciful Resort. The two seemed to be disagreeing over a suggestion that Hurley had made to Mike. He wanted Mike to be in charge, more hands-on at Southern Fanciful Resort. Mike shook his head as the two men walked towards the silver truck.

*   *   *

As Hurley drove down Lewis Road towards Highway 177 Mike agreed to take the job.

Hurley grinned and said, "I figured you would."

Mike looked at him nodded his head yes, then looked back out of the passenger window. The two didn't say a word to one another as Hurley pulled up in front of Hank's to eat lunch.

Hurley turned off the truck's engine and looked at Mike. "You hungry?"

"Yes, sir," Mike replied with a smile.

"Well hell let's go eat." Hurley said opening his door.

They got out and closed the doors of the truck. As the two walked towards the glass door Mike asked Hurley if he thought that they'd have another encounter with Maynard Phillips. The two laughed as they went into Hank's.

*   *   *

It was going on 9 o'clock that night when Mike saw a set of beaming headlights pulling into the parking lot of Southern Fanciful Resort. He stood up from his office chair, situated behind the reception desk, and quickly brushed himself with his open hand.

"Good evening!" Mike said as a young man entered through the front door.

"Same to you," the man said as he stood at the clerk's counter. "Everything in town was filled up."

"Yes, probably so. So what will it be? Single or double bed and how long?" Mike asked.

"Single and a week," the man said, putting his driver's license and insurance card on the wooden countertop.

Mike picked up the cards and filled out the registration form for the man. "All right, Mr. Clark. Here's your cards back, and if you will please sign this at the bottom.

Matthew Clark put the cards away in his wallet and signed the registration form.

"That'll be three hundred and fifteen dollars," said Mike. "You'll be in Room 1."

Clark gave Mike three crisp one hundred dollar bills with a crumpled and torn twenty.

"Here's your change," Mike said, giving Clark a five back.

Clark got the key and walked out, then pulled his car over to Room1, turned off the headlights. Mike heard the sound of two car doors slamming shut, but he sat back down in his chair. Before morning Mike had put another couple, Jon and

Barbara Hall, in Room 5 for a four day stay.

CHAPTER THREE

Dawn broke the next day. It was Saturday morning.

Matthew Clark had unpacked his luggage into Room 1. Jan

was still sleeping as Barbara walked around sightseeing.

Mike went outside, looked down at the lake, then towards

the motel when loud music made him look towards the

driveway at Room 1. Mike spotted a red Jeep with four

passengers pulling up to him. As they approached, he could

tell it was two males and two females. The male driver got

out. "I'm Tim Shaw," he said. "I booked a couple of rooms

yesterday through your website."

"Oh, yeah," Mike replied, leading the way into the office.

After the paperwork was done, Tim pulled the red Jeep in front of room 10 and killed the engine. The four unloaded from the Jeep talking and laughing loudly.

"Hey, Lee," Tim said, "you and Ashley can get Room 9. Susan and me will stay in Room 10." He handed Lee the key to Room 9.

*   *   *

Everyone had settled in by the time Hurley pulled up to the office building. He got out, shut the truck door, and went into the office and found Mike seated behind the clerk's desk watching television. Mike was startled by his voice and stood up out of the office chair. The two men talked for over an hour, then Hurley got the Room 6 key and left out of the office. He drove his truck to the parking space for Room 6, got out, and looked around the grounds as he made his way to Room 6. Everyone was down at the lake swimming, except for Matthew Clark who sat on a wooden bench, looking toward the lake. The swimmers splashed each other with water, dove off of the dock, and some talked while treading water.

Matthew Clark grilled at Room 1, as Barbara was trying to persuade Matthew's wife, Sara, to go swimming with her at 8 o'clock that night. Lee, Tim, Ashley, and Susan were also grilling and drinking beer. Hurley, however, never came out of Room 6. Barbara walked in flip flops down the pebble trail towards the lake by herself, as Sara watched from the porch of Room1, within the smoke from the grill. Barbara slid her flip flops off at the edge of the water and walked into the warm water to cool off. She'd been in the lake for about five minutes when she looked towards the bank where her flip flops had been. She saw a large, hulking person standing and watching her.

"Come on you guys," she called, "not this shit." But when the figure neither spoke nor moved, she swam closer to get a better look.

She stopped even with the end of the dock and wiped the water from her face, but the large figure was gone.

A hand grabbed Barbara tightly around her throat and dragged her beneath the surface of the lake.

*   *   *

Sara was walking down the pebbled trail to the lake. She walked onto the wooden dock past Barbara's flip flops, and stopped at the edge of the dock. She called out Barbara's name, but received no reply.

"Um," Sara mumbled to herself. "Must have passed her at some point."

She called once more before turning back towards the motel up on the hill. Sara looked up from the dock and walked towards the lit-up trail. At the end of the dock she heard a twig snap nearby and stopped.

"Barbara!" she called. "Come on out. You're not scaring anybody."

Sara began walking towards the tree line. Leaves on the branched above her rustled quickly, and she threw her attention toward the sound.

"That you Barbara?" she asked, squinting up into the tree.

She stepped back then, intent on heading back to her room. But what she saw through the trees made her gasp: a huge, hideous, burnt man, wearing torn Navy blue pants and a matching long sleeved shirt. Green moss, algae, and leeches grew in clusters on his skin, and loose wads of grey Spanish moss, hung from his scalp as if it were his hair.

Before she could speak, the hideous man quickly pulled a hatchet from the metal ring of the tool belt. The hatchet flew through the woods, deftly missing every tree, branch, and bush, until it stopped in Sara's skull.

CHAPTER FOUR

White lightning flashed in the Eastern sky, revealing a growing thunderhead that moved toward the motel. It was moving Northwest, towards the motel.

"Has anyone seen Barbara?" Tim asked.

"No, I can't find Sara either," replied Matthew. "I know that when I was grilling Barbara came over and asked Sara to go swimming with her. Hell, that's been an hour ago."

"I'll go and get everyone together in the office if you want to go on to the lake," said Tim.

"All right, let me grab a flashlight out of my room," Matthew replied.

The two men went in different directions. The storm was now getting more intense. Tim gathered the others up in the office with Mike Jones, where he explained his wife and Matthew's wife were missing.

"There are six of us in here," Lee suggested. "I say that we pair up into three groups and get our asses out there searching."

"I agree," said Susan. "Nothing's getting done in here by talking."

*   *   *

Matthew Clark was searching around the lake with a flashlight in his hand. The only thing he'd seen was

Barbara's flip flops. He'd called out to Barbara and Sara occasionally. The wind blew constantly. The others had grabbed some flashlights and paired into three groups. Tim and Lee paired together, Mike Jones with Tim, and the two women Susan and Ashley. The two women walked Lewis Road with Mike Jones. Tim and Lee went westward. As Matthew Clark was at the dock calling for the women, Hatchetface walked out of the woods. Clark never noticed him. Hatchetface stood behind Clark, and when Clark turned, his face bumped into Hatchetface's chest. As he began to yell, Hatchetface grabbed inside of Clark's mouth with both hands and pulled.

*   *   *

Tim and Lee had walked two hundred yards from the motel and into the woods. The only thing that they heard was leaving rustling on the trees. Hatchetface turned towards the motel to see flashlights shining in the woods on both ends of the motel and walked towards them in the woods.

"Lee, you go on ahead and circle back," Tim said. "I'll go down towards the lake and meet back with you at the motel."

"All right," Lee said. "Be careful."

The two separated in the woods and walked their planned routes. Hatchetface pulled his hatchet from the tool belt and made four swift whacks into thin sapling. The noise alerted Tim, and he ran quickly to see the a perfectly formed stake standing out of the ground where the sapling had once stood.. He was breathing fast as he looked around in the woods for someone or any movement. After he hadn't

spotted or heard anyone, he bent over and placed his balled

up fists on his knees, trying to catch his breath. Hatchetface

walked up behind Tim and grabbed him up off of the ground.

The flashlight dropped to the ground, and Hatchetface

impaled Tim onto the makeshift stake, which exited out of

his chest.

*   *   *

Lee was walking back towards the motel when a flash of

white lightning flashed across the sky. It was followed by a

loud rumble of thunder, and then it began to rain hard and

steady. Lee stopped walking and looked around with his

flashlight. All that he heard was the rain hitting the leaves

and the ground. The wind had eased now to a light breeze.

Lee turned back towards the motel to see a huge, imposing figure blocking his path.

"So you are real," Lee said. He'd barely finished uttering the words before Hatchetface punched him in the chest.

The flashlight fell to the ground as Hatchetface stuck his hands in Lee's broken sternum and ripped him apart.

CHAPTER FIVE

The others four had regrouped and retreated into the office as Hatchetface looked at the motel from the woods. The rain fell harder.

"So tell us more about this about that crazy story you were talking about," Ashley said.

Mike Jones sat himself down in the office chair behind the clerk's desk.

"Nothing much to tell, really," Mike said. "It's just an old story the people around here tell to keep their kids from sneaking off in the woods and—you know—being kids. He's known as Hatchetface, and supposedly, he owns all of this land. He was killed by some of his friends years ago, and he came back to life with superhuman strength and all that shit. He's pretty much indestructible. And he kills everybody that doesn't belong here." this place, thinned the trees and built it up. For what reason and why still gets me." Mike said.

"I don't believe in monsters," said Ashley, "but if I wanted to be a serial killer, that would be a great cover." She reached for the landline phone on the receptionist's desk. "I'm calling the police."

"Have at it," said Mike. "I need to go and check on my friend in Room 6. You two stay here till I get back."

Mike to the front door and looked out to see rain falling within the lights out front of the hotel. Lightning still lit up the night sky and thunder rumbled in the distance now. Mike put his right hand on the golden doorknob and opened the front door of the hotel.

*   *   *

Mike splashed his way through puddle in the asphalt on his way to Room 6. He knocked on the door at first, then balled his fist and beat it against the door. He had only struck the door a few times when it opened slightly. He pushed it open to reveal a pitch black room.

"Hurley," Mike yelled. "You in here?"

He flipped on the light switch. The room was thrashed. The bed had been flipped over onto the floor, and shards of glass from the mirror over the dresser now littered the carpet.

Mike walked towards the bathroom slowly. As he neared

the bed, Hatchetface stepped out of the bathroom. Mike

back stepped toward the door, but Hatchetface pulled his

hunting knife from its leather sheath. Mike turned and ran

out into the rain with Hatchetface quickly following him.

Mike jumped the chain link fence of the cemetery and hid

behind a tombstone. Hatchetface entered into the cemetery

and scanned among the tombstones for his prey. He focused

on the tombstone which Mike hid behind. But then, out of

nowhere, Hatchetface seemed to lose interest, and left the

cemetery through the gate. Puzzled, Mike jumped to his feet

and climbed over the fence at the rear of the cemetery. He

dropped to the wet ground on the other side, letting the

gridwork of the chain link fence rattle behind him as he

bolted into the darkness. He found a small clearing behind

the motel and stopped to catch his breath. But as he looked

up and opened his mouth to drink some of the rain water,

Hatchetface stood behind him, gripping his hunting knife.

Hatchetface quickly grabbed Mike's head and put the knife

in the back of his mouth and pulled the knife towards

himself. Mike's face was severed off as he and his face fell

onto the wet ground. Hatchetface put the knife into its

sheath as lightning flashed in the sky followed by rumbling

thunder. He picked up Mike's body, put it over his shoulder

and walked to a quicksand pit. Hatchetface forcefully threw

Mike's body in the quicksand and watched as the body

vanished.

ERNEST ROBERSON SR-

CHAPTER SIX

Ashley had found some hairspray in the lost and found bin behind the front desk, along with a lighter.

"I'm scared," Susan said.

"Listen, there is no need of losing our minds," Ashley replied, sitting in the office chair behind the desk. "This may all be a joke and it's on us. So just pull yourself together."

Lightning continued to flash and thunder rumbled outside.

"Then why did you call the police?" Susan asked.

"Just in case."

"But what if they're dead?"

"Who?"

"All of them," said Susan, staring out of the front door. "What if we're the only ones left?"

Ashley stood.

She opened the door at the end of the receptionist counter, crossed the lobby and locked the front door. On her way back, she pointed at Susan. "Just in case," she said. "You stay here. I'm going out to round up some supplies. Look everywhere in here and see what you can find."

"What am I looking for?"

"Anything."

*　　*　　*

Ashley returned with an unmounted tire she'd found in the back of the silver truck out front. She leaned the tire against the wall and walked behind the clerk's desk to find a white jug sitting on the counter beside a small fire extinguisher.

Susan pointed to it. "It's gasoline," she said. "Will that work? You know—just in case."

Ashley laughed. "Absolutely. If we fuck up and catch the place on fire at least we can put it out with the fire extinguisher.

Susan forced a laugh and brushed past Ashley.

"Where are you going?" Ashley asked.

"I just need some air."

"Don't go too far," Ashley said. She stared out of the front windows, trying to pick out any movement through the rain.

*   *   *

Susan had only been gone for a few moments when Ashley thought she caught something moving outside. The rain was too heavy, so she squinted and leaned across the counter. Just then, a body slammed against the front door and dropped, crumpled over in a sitting position.

Ashley jumped back from the counter, then hid behind it. After what seemed like hours to her, she stood up and peeked over the counter.

The rain fell, but otherwise she saw no movement out front.

With the can of hairspray in one hand and the lighter in the other, she took small, tentative steps through the lobby. She stood close enough to the glass to recognize Susan's body, but she did not scream when she saw that a bloody stump was all that remained of her friend's head.

She shook all over and took a few steps back. Tears ran form her eyes, although she did not cry. Instead she staggered back behind the desk as though she'd been drugged and fumbled with the telephone until she remembered how to dial an outside line. Just as the police dispatcher picked up on the other end, the lights went out.

"Hello?" she whispered into the receiver. "Are you there?"

She held the phone to her ear for a moment longer, even though she heard no dial tone.

After she'd placed the receiver back in its cradle, she pulled out her cell phone. She blinked a few times, staring at the words "No Service" at the top of the screen.

CHAPTER SEVEN

The little digital clock beside her read 3 AM SUNDAY. She lay behind the counter, covered with a comforter she'd found in one of the closets, still gripping the can of hairspray and the lighter. She'd locked the side door Susan had used earlier. She had not slept, only closed her eyes.

Even with a light drizzle outside the thunder sounded like someone beating on metal trash cans. The front door flew off of its hinges and slid across the tile floor of the lobby, almost touching the receptionist counter before it ceased its sliding. Ashley sprang to her feet to find Hatchetface in the doorway.

"Oh my God," she whispered. "It's all true."

They stood that way, silently facing one another. Ashley was the first to move. She grabbed up the small fire extinguisher from the desk, leaped across the desk, and ran toward Hatchetface, brandishing the fire extinguisher in both hands. As if in surprise, Hatchetface tilted his head, unsure of what to make of this petite woman, completely helpless in the face of his immense strength. Without thinking, she leaped at him and swung the fire extinguisher. The blow turned Hatchetface's head to the side, and he stumbled once, then fell to the tile floor. But Ashley had landed wrong and twisted her ankle. She fell, dropping the fire extinguisher, but pushed herself back up. The pain had not yet set in, but she made sure not to put all of her weight on her injured foot as she opened the door that lead behind the counter.

She grunted a few times, then managed to roll the tire out into the lobby. When she'd made it halfway to Hatchetface, she lost her hold on the tire and fell. On the ground, she looked across the cold tile, checking to see if Hatchetface had moved. She made it to her feet once more, then continued to roll the tire. Once she'd made it to her feet, she pulled the tire back up, but found that she could not keep her weight of her injured ankle if she there was any chance of maneuvering the tire. The pain had begun to set it, but it was only a dull ache now. She pushed through it until she stood beside the monstrous body.

Just then, Hatchetface's hand twitched.

Ashley spotted the fire extinguisher beside her. She dropped the tire onto Hatchetface's chest, took up the fire extinguisher, then dropped to her knees beside Hatchetface. She brough the fire extinguisher up above her head and slammed it down over and over as hard as she could, crashing it into his face until her arms burned.

He did not move.

She threw the fire extinguisher down, then grabbed the back of his head. She strained and snatched until she'd positioned the tire over Hatchetface's body, then stood. The pain had grown, and she felt her ankle throbbing as she hopped back to the counter. She brought back the jug of gasoline and the lighter.

She unscrewed the cap and doused the tire and the body, then poured out a trail of gasoline that ended at the reception counter. She poured another trail up to the front door, just out of reach of the rain that blew in.

The wind had died down just enough for her to light the small lighter.

"Go back to hell, you son of a bitch," she said, the bent and lit the trail of gasoline that led to the tire atop Hatchetface's body.

*　　*　　*

Sharp, hot jolts of pain stabbed her ankle as she ran through the parking lot.

She'd almost made it to the first vehicle when the explosion ripped through the office.

The rain had not let up, and it took her a moment to make out the silver Ford just a few steps away. Spent, she let down the tailgate the tailgate and laid down in the bed of the truck, resting her bad ankle on the tailgate.

She closed her eyes, letting the cold rain fall on her as she listened to the gentle crackle of what she knew to be the fire blazing in the office.

She opened her eyed as she slid out of the truck. Hatchetface stood her up in front of him. She gaped at him—the bald, burned away face and scalp, the charred flesh, and the scalded leeches that somehow continued to writhe on his chest and arms. He spun her around and bent her over the tailgate,   making two quick and deep cuts down the sides of her spine with his hunting knife. He put the knife away, then pulled her ribs apart from her spine and pulled out her lungs. She collapsed face down onto the wet asphalt as blood surrounded her. Hatchetface walked past Room 10, then down to the cemetery.

ERNEST ROBERSON SR-

CHAPTER EIGHT

The storm had passed, and the sun broke the darkness. Police sirens echoed coming up Lewis Road off of Highway 177. When the two white patrol cars stopped in front of Southern Fanciful Resort Motel they feared for the worst. Sergeant Andrew Dixon got on the C.B. radio as the other three looked around.

"This is Sergeant Dixon. We're 10-23. Send the fire department."

"At the resort?" the dispatcher asked.

"10-4," Sgt. Dixon replied.

Corporal Mullins shook his head at Sgt. Dixon using the radio. "What do you make of it?" he asked.

"It's a damn mess already, and we ain't even seen it."

"Sergeant!" yelled a young female officer. Sgt. Dixon and Corp. Mullins looked over to the officer, who stood beside a silver Ford truck. "We have a body."

"Shit in the sunshine," Sgt. Dixon muttered under his breath. He held the C.B. receiver to his mouth once more. "Sergeant Dixon again. Send an ambulance, and a coroner down to the resort. Over." He threw the receiver back into his car. "I'll be goddamned, Mullins."

"Me, too," the Corporal replied, and followed Sgt. Dixon to the silver truck.

*　　*　　*

"You all right, Sierra?" Sgt. Dixon asked the female officer. "You don't look so good."

"Yes, sir," said Sierra. She kept her back to the bed of the truck. "Just never seen something like that before."

"In all my years of doing this, I haven't either." He looked to the other officers standing around the truck. "Don't touch nothing until the paramedics get here. Is the perimeter secure yet? No? The what the hell are y'all doing standing around? Get my perimeter secured."

ERNEST ROBERSON SR-

CHAPTER NINE

Cadet Officer Pak, which was of Korean descendent, walked down to the lake on the pebbled trail. He searched the branch line and the white sandy bank before walking onto the dock. He looked out over the lake and listened to the birds chirp and sing. He then turned and walked off of the dock. As he walked in the sand towards the trail an unidentified person walking in the woods to his left stopped him. He pulled his gun from its holster and walked towards the person, but when he got close enough to see, he realized no one was there. He searched within the tree line for a few more minutes. When he turned to walk towards the trail, he stood face to face with Hatchetface. Hatchetface picked him up by the throat and threw him against the thick trunk of a nearby oak. Blood spurted from Pak's mouth as he hit the tree, then crumpled onto the ground.

*   *   *

Sierra had to get the other room keys out of the front office. She hadn't found anything out of place except for signs of a struggle in Room 6. Sierra searched the room for any piece of evidence that would and could be a clue to what happened at Southern Fanciful Resort. Corporal Mullins walked into the room.

"You find anything that might help us figure out this mess?" he said.

"Where would I start?" Sierra said. "This is way more messed up than anything we've seen in years. But I think that whoever was in this room knows what's going on."

"What makes you think that?"

"Well, look at it. This is the only room that's been trashed. That's no accident."

"Possibly, Have you seen that Cadet Chin-Ho lately?" Corporal Mullins asked turning to walk out of the doorway.

"No, sir but I do believe he went down to the lake," Sierra replied.

"All right then," Corporal Mullins said, walking out of the door.

* * *

The door to Room 6 shut as Sierra searched the bathroom.

"You back so soon?" she asked as she was looking around.

No one answered.

"Corporal Mullins, is that you?"

Still no one answered. As Sierra was walking out of the bathroom the Hatchetface threw her against the shower wall, shattering the ceramic square tiles. Hatchetface walked towards Sierra as she lay on the shower floor and grabbed her by the hair. Once on her feet, Hatchetface slammed her face through the sheetrock wall. Sierra reached and got her mace. Hatchetface threw her into the wall facing the bathroom door and Sierra fell onto the carpet. As he walked towards her out of the bathroom Sierra positioned herself in

a sitting position facing him and sprayed the mace.

Hatchetface grabbed his face with both hands as he

stumbled around. Sierra used all of the mace in the container

on him. She was now standing up again. Hatchetface

continued to stumble but managed to grab Sierra by her

brown shirt. She unbuttoned the buttons which Hatchetface

didn't tear off. She was now in her brown pants and white

bra. Hatchetface could see again and lunged at her. Once

more, he clasped his right hand around her neck and threw

her into the sheetrock wall, bursting it with the impact of her

body.

*   *   *

Sierra woke up handcuffed to the headboard. She was too weak to scream as Hatchetface stood to her right beside the bed.

"No, please," Sierra begged as Hatchetface pulled the hatchet from his tool belt.

"You don't have to do this," Sierra said.

Hatchetface grabbed Sierra by her blond hair and put the hatchet in an upward position in her mouth. He held the hatchet with his left hand and her hair with his right hand, then slammed her head down, splitting her head a the jaw line. He put the hatchet into the ring on the tool belt and dropped her upper decapitated head onto the floor.

CHAPTER TEN

Sergeant Dixon was on the C.B. radio again.

"What's the hold up?" Sergeant Dixon asked

harshly.

"Sorry, Sergeant," the female dispatcher replied. "A

gas truck exploded, so all of your back up and paramedics

are tending to that. They're coming as soon as they get it

under control."

"10-4" Sergeant Dixon said, throwing the C.B radio

into the car.

"It's Hatchetface," said Corporal Mullins, getting off the hood of the patrol car, "and you know it."

"Bullshit. There's a perfectly rational—"

Sgt. Dixon pulled his pistol and trained it on a man dressed in a blue suit.

"Hands up!" Sgt. Dixon commanded. "Up!"

Hurley Edenfield stood with his hands up. "Sorry if I scared you, officers. I'm the owner here."

"You'll forgive me if I don't take your word for it."

"Of course not. Let me get my wallet out of my jacket pocket."

"Slow as Christmas, mister," said Corporal Mullins, standing beside the sergeant with his pistol drawn.

Hurley reached and pulled out his brown leather wallet. "Here you go check my license."

"Mullins," said Sgt. Dixon, holstering his weapon. "I'll put him in my car I'll run his ID. We can't take any chances."

"Yes, sir. I thought we'd hear back from Pak or Sierra. I'll go see if they've run into trouble."

"Go on, then. Keep your head on a swivel, Mullins."

"Always," Mullins said, walked towards the lake on the pebbled trail.

* * *

Sergeant Dixon got in his patrol car and got the C.B. radio. Nothing had come back negative about Hurley

Edenfield, not even a citation on his criminal record.

Sergeant Dixon laid the C.B. down in the passenger seat and

got out of the car. He opened the door to let Hurley out of

the car.

"Is there anything that you know that I need to know

about? Its bloodshed out here and only one body has been

found. Who's vehicles are these?"

"I don't know," Hurley replied.

"Is one of them yours?"

"That silver truck is."

"So you don't know whose body that is behind your

truck?" Sgt. Dixon asked.

"Body? No, sir. I don't know anything about any bodies."

"Bodies? Now what makes you think there's more than one, Mr. Hurley?"

The C.B. crackled. "Sergeant Dixon," the female dispatcher said.

Sergeant Dixon grabbed up the mic. "Go ahead, dispatch."

"I ran the I.D. you gave me.

"And?"

Sergeant Dixon kept his attention fixed on Hurley in backseat.

"He's clean. No priors. Not even a traffic violation."

"10-4."

"There's one more thing, Sergeant."

"What's that?"

"I know you don't believe in the Hatchetface stories, but when I was running the I.D., I came across some records that you might find interesting."

"Jesus," Dixon said, without pressing the mic button for the C.B. "They just won't quit with this Hatchetface stuff." He pressed the mic button. "Let me have it, dispatch."

"The story goes that John Lewis, Jr. is supposedly Hatchetface. Everybody says John Lewis, Sr. was his father, right?"

"Yeah. Get to the point, please."

"Yes, sir. I have a Hurley Edenfield listed as the father of John Lewis, Jr. It's the same John Lewis, Jr. that went missing back in the day. If those stories are true—"

"They're not."

"But if they are, then that accounts for the murder of John Lewis, Sr. a while back."

"How's that?"

"Because John Lewis, Sr. wasn't his father."

Hurley did not move. He looked past Sgt, Dixon to some fixed point in the parking lot, flashed a quick, smug grin, then regained his composure.

"Thanks, dispatch, but I'm not in the mood to hash out conspiracy theories about a made up killer. Let me know when you have something concrete."

"Sorry, Sergeant. Will do."

"Now look here, Mr. Edenfield," Sgt. Dixon said. "I know you know something about what happened here. We can talk about it here, or we can go back to—"

Sgt. Dixon tried to speak, but thick, dark blood gurgled out of his mouth. He looked down, eyes wide with surprise, to find the head of a large hatchet growing out of his sternum. The C.B. mic dangled from the opened driver door of the squad car, bouncing on its curled cord just shy of hitting the asphalt.

"Sgt. Dixon?" the female dispatcher called over the C.B. "Your backup is on the way. They pulled some folks from another department to help out with the tanker."

Sgt. Dixon collapsed. Hatchetface stood beside the car, severely burned, but showing no signs of pain. He looked into the backseat at Hurley, who simply nodded at the C.B. on the dash of the car. As if on cue, Hatchetface reached inside and crushed the C.B. with his bare hand.

ERNEST ROBERSON SR-

CHAPTER ELEVEN

Corporal Mullins was walking back up the trail towards the motel on the hill when he got the feeling that someone was watching him. He brushed it off, and continued walking with his shoulders back and head up as he approached the patrol cars. But when he got the Sgt. Dixon's car, his body language changed. Both doors were open, and what was left of the C.B. lay on the ground beside the car. Both doors on the driver's side of the door were open, but he saw no sign of Hurley or Sgt. Dixon. The asphalt had only been laid a few months before, and it took him a moment for him to make out the dark spatter of blood beside the car.

Quietly, he took a single step back and unholstered his weapon. He made no sudden movements.

Weapon drawn, he searched the other cars, only to find their radios had been destroyed, as well. He backtracked, hoping to find Pak or Sierra. He assumed he would not find Sgt. Dixon. As he was searching along the chain link fence of the cemetery, the low wail of sirens came to him from the main road, carrying through the still and quiet morning. He took a deep breath, and sighed. He returned his pistol to its holster.

*   *   *

He made his way back to the parking lot. The sirens were very close now, but the uneasy feeling of being watched came over him once more and he turned around to find Hatchetface only an arm's length away.   Before

Mullins could draw his gun, Hatchetface grabbed him and carried him behind the office. Mullins struggled and fought but couldn't break himself free from Hatchetface's grip. As two white patrol cars following each other sped into the driveway and stopped behind Sgt. Dixon's car, Hatchetface released Mullins. The officer grabbed his gun from the holster, but Hatchetface snatched it away with impossible speed, then stabbed Mullins in the abdomen with his hunting knife. Hatchetface ejected the magazine, then dropped the gun onto. Wounded, Mullins half-ran, half-staggered back toward the parking lot. Hatchetface followed, stalking his prey without a sound. But as Mullins rounded the corner, Hatchetface lodged the magazine into Corporal Mullins neck, and he staggered on into the parking lot and up the driveway. The ambulance never saw him. The impact crushed his organs and left him in a bloody heap on the ground.

Once more, Hatchetface blended into the woods. For now, his job was done. His land was once again safe. But he stalks the area still, waiting to protect his home by any means necessary.

About the Author:

Ernest Roberson, Sr. was born in Glenwood, GA, and has lived there for most of his life. His works include a book of poetry titled *The Heart Speaks* (2019), sixteen short stories that have appeared in *Blood Moon Rising* magazine (2015-2020), and a novella, *Damnation* (2020).

Follow Ernest on his writing journey:

Facebook: Ernest Roberson, Sr.

Instagam: robersonsr.ernest

Twitter: @thewriter1976

Amazon: amazon.com/author/ernestrobersonsr

ERNEST ROBERSON SR-